Far to Go, A Story of the Oregon Trail

by

Frances Beryl Vance

ISBN: 978-0-578-81190-1

GOODBY! GOODBY!

"Li-i-b-by. Libby Ann. Where are you?"

Libby snuggled deep into her nest of hay. She could hear her mother calling but she did not answer. She pulled her cat Greyboy tighter in her arms and lay very still. The early morning sun poured into the barn loft, lighting up the shadows and warming the early April chill. Libby listened to the voices of her family down below as they. loaded their covered wagon for the long trip west to Oregon.

"Jesse, bring the cattle through the gate and drive them behind the freight wagon," Papa shouted.

Libby heard the rattle of tin dishes and iron cooking pots as they were put into the grub box in the back of the wagon.

" Is everybody here and ready to go?" Papa asked.

"Libby is missing," answered her older sister, Nancy.

"It's past daylight. We should get started. Nancy, go find her."

"Li-i-by. Elizabeth Ann Campbell, answer me," Nancy

called.

Libby curled herself into a ball holding Greyboy in her arms. Greyboy had belonged to her for as long as she could remember and she was sad to have to leave him behind with Grandma. She squeezed her eyes shut and stayed silent. She wanted just a little longer to hold her pet.

Libby where are you?" Nancy called again. "Libby, if you don't show yourself you are in a whole lot of trouble. We are all ready to go."

Libby lay quiet in the hay. She would try to slip out of the loft and creep up to the wagon. She couldn't let anybody know that she had been hiding in the hayloft all the time.

"Libby Ann," called Grandma from below. Climb down from the loft. You know I will take good care of Greyboy. Say good-by to him and come down now."

Libby didn't want to make Grandma cry like she had when Papa told her the family was going to Oregon. She rubbed her cheek against Greyboy's soft fur then put him on a high mound of hay and quickly climbed down the pole ladder from the loft. Grandma reached for the straws sticking out from Libby's dark braids and smoothed the top of her head.

"There," she said. "You look fresh as a daisy. Nobody could

guess you've been in the hayloft this morning." She took Libby's hand and they walked out of the barn and up to the big blue wagon with its giant red wheels standing just outside Grandma and Grandpa's front door.

"Here she is everybody," Grandma called." And she has been ready to go all along. "

Nancy stomped her foot, Mama looked relieved and Papa pushed back the brim of his hat. The corners of his mouth turned down and his forehead wrinkled as if things were not right but he turned toward the big wagon and said, "Let's get going folks."

Mama climbed up to the wagon seat with three year old Ben. His chubby little legs barely hung over the edge of the wagon seat where he sat between Mama and Papa. Papa walked back to the freight wagon. He checked the four oxen to make sure their yokes and chains were fastened.

"Do you have everything tied down tight, Will?" he asked?

Will, the the ox team driver, stroked his beard and said, "I got it all tight and ship shape Mr. Callahan. This freight wagon is a rarin ta go. En' I should know. I done been over them mountains onest before an I say she's ready for em."

Libby stood beside the wagon watching as Jesse, her fifteen year old brother, brought the herd of bawling cattle through the corral gate and up behind the freight wagon. He rode his black mare, Maggie, back and forth in a cloud of dust to keep the cattle from straying.

Papa checked the four mules hitched to the big family wagon. The wagon box had two levels. The one underneath was filled with supplies and tools. Wooden boards covered them and made a floor for the top of the box which had beds, clothes, a lantern, Mama's sewing box and spinning wheel and slickers for keeping the men dry. Papa and Jesse's rifles hung inside on pegs fastened to the bows that held the wagon's big white cover. At the back of the wagon was the grub box and the butter churn.

Grandpa and Grandma stood outside their front gate watching. Libby looked back at them standing in the dust stirred up by the milling cattle. Bibby, Grandpa's brown shepherd dog, danced excitedly until Grandpa reached down and patted her head.

Libby waited for Papa to climb up to the seat of the family wagon but he turned and looked back at Grandma and Grandpa and called, "Goodby, Ma and Pa. Take care of yourselves. We will write." Everyone waved to Grandma and Grandpa.

Libby felt tears on her cheeks. It was sad to leave Grandpa and Grandma. They were too old to make the long trip to Oregon and she knew that she might never see them again. Grandpa stood very still then pulled his red handkerchief from his pocket and wiped the dust and tears from his cheeks. Grandma smiled and waved then took her glasses off her nose and with her fingers scattered any sign of unhappy tears.

"Libby, Libby," she called above the noise of the cattle. "Come get the bonnets I made for you."

Libby ran past the the big blue wagon then straight to Grandma.

"Oh, Grandma, I forgot our bonnets."

"Here they are dear. You left them on the kitchen table when you helped your mother pack the dishes."

Libby reached her arms around Grandma's waist and squeezed tight. "Thank you, thank you Grandma."

"Don't cry Libby. If the Lord's willing we'll see you again. Now run back and give your sister her bonnet. Don't let the hot sun spoil your skin."

Libby ran back to the big wagon and handed a dark blue calico sunbonnet to Nancy and put on her yellow, one.

Papa waved one last time to Grandpa and Grandma then climbed up to the wagon seat. Facing the long road ahead he shook the leather lines of the mules harness and called out, "Getty up Toby. You Tucker get in there. Get up Prince. Get along Barney."

The big mules moved ahead pulling the heavy wagon to begin the long journey toward their new home in Oregon.

"Giddy up you stragglers," called Will and he cracked his long leather whip. "Gee Baldy. Get in there Clementine. Get on there Tansy and Speckle," Will called as he walked along the four yoke of oxen pulling the freight wagon filled with meat, flour, coffee, sugar, meal and tools they would need in Oregon.

Libby walked with Nancy beside the family wagon. She pulled her grey wool shawl tight around her butternut colored linsey woolsey dress that reached to the tops of her heavy, leather shoes.

"Nancy, how far is it to Oregon? Is it a long way?"

"Yes Libby. Papa says it is two thousand miles to Oregon from Grandpa's farm here in Missouri. That is farther than you have ever been, farther even than you can imagine. We won't be getting there for six months or so. Stretch your legs and keep up and don't get far from the wagon. We will be camping out tonight before we get to Independence. Papa says that is the jumping off place."

"What's the Jumping Off Place, Nancy?"

"The Jumping Off Place is where the wagons gather to cross the Missouri river and start the trip across the wild country to Oregon."

" Are there wild animals there?"

"Yes. There will be a lot of wild animals there and Indians . You will have to listen to Mama and Papa and do as they say. It won't be a time to be doing things on your own, Libby."

"What do you mean doing things on my own? Won't I do any chores or help take care of Ben?"

"Of course you will have chores but you can't be going off by yourself, forgetting what you've been told.

"I wish I was seventeen like you Nancy. I could stay up at night with the grown ups and listen to them talk. I am just twelve years old and not very important. The only thing I can do is run for this and run for that. Do you think I will ever be important Nancy?"

"Of course you will Libby, but try to do as Mama and Papa tell you. Next year you will be thirteen and that is almost a young lady."

Libby stopped and dug her toe in the dust and wondered. All the way to Oregon would things be the same? Nobody would notice her until they wanted her to run get something . When she tried to help Mama, she would say, "Libby dear, step out of the way while I am busy." Papa warned, "Don't get too close to the animals," and Jesse sometimes yelled, "You aren't old enough to ride a horse so stay out of Maggie's way."

"Libby." called Nancy. "Hurry, so we don't get too far behind."

Libby looked up the road where her sister stood waiting. The wagons had moved far ahead. She ran, making the dust puff out from under her feet as she hurried to reach her sister.

All morning Libby walked with Nancy beside the family wagon. It's big blue box and red wheels rolled on until they stopped for the nooning. Mama spread an old quilt on the ground and laid out chicken and some fresh bread that Grandma had baked. They took some cold water from the little spring that bubbled out of a grass covered bank. The family sat on the grass for a rest . Will stretched out on his back and covered his face with his hat. Libby moved over to sit beside him. She was hoping he would tell one of his tales about Oregon.

"Will," she asked, "Are there wild animals in Oregon?"

"You bet, Missy," Will answered. "You'll see some big old grey wolves and shaggy old buffalo long before you even get to Oregon."

"Should I be afraid of them?"

"Not likely they will be close enough to hurt ye. Now go to your Ma. I aim ta take me a little snooze fore we pull out. Them old oxen are mighty stubborn sometimes and they caused me a heap o trouble this mornin."

Libby scooted across the grass and sat watching some small yellow butterflies. She felt the warm noon sun on her face. She gathered her shawl around her, lay down and fell asleep.She woke up when she heard Papa call.

"Let's load up."

***

Libby skipped along beside Nancy as the little caravan moved on. She looked for early wild flowers along the road There were new leaves popping out on the trees and fat robins hopped about in the grass looking for worms. I know what we can do." Nancy said. We can name the trees that we see along the way. I know there are several different kinds along the road.

I"ll go first. Look, there is a red oak tree. Now it's your turn.

Libby searched the roadside and up in front of the wagon a small tree spread out it branches in a wide circle and on the limbs were tiny red buds. She pointed straight ahead. “There’s a red bud tree and it's blooming.

'Yes, it is a redbud and very pretty one too. That tells us spring is here,” answered Nancy.

They looked for trees to name until Libby grew tired and pulled her sunbonnet back to cool her head from the warm afternoon sun. She stuck out her chin and pulled her feet from one step to the next determined to keep up with her older sister. She wouldn't be a straggler. She would show everybody she could keep up with the wagon.

She walked down the dusty road until she grew tired and pulled her sunbonnet back to cool her head from the warm afternoon sun. She stuck out her chin and pulled her feet from one step to the next, determined to keep up with Nancy. She wouldn't be a straggler. She would show everybody that she could keep up

The wagons rumbled down the road, the cattle bawled and Jesse urged his horse Maggie after the ones that strayed away. Will cracked his big whip now and then to make the oxen pull over steep banks and bumps in the road. The road seemed so long and Libby was so tired of walking . When she thought she could not take another step Papa called.

"Whoa!"

He drove the mules and the blue wagon into a grassy meadow surrounded by big oak trees that were close to a small stream.

"Time to camp for the night," he said.

The sky had turned red and the big round sun hung just above the treetops. Libby sat down on the grass, leaned against a big tree trunk, and stretched her tired legs out in front of her. She untied her sunbonnet and laid it carefully on the grass. She watched as Papa and Jesse put up a big tent and Mama built a cooking fire under the tripod which held the iron cooking pot. Will took the heavy yokes off the oxen and let them graze with the other cattle. Nancy took the old quilt and tin dishes and cups out of the grub box and set a place for all the family. Everyone had a job and everyone was busy except Libby.

She looked for something to do. Nobody seemed to need her help. She pulled her knees up and hugged them then lay her head on them to rest. She was startled by a hissing sound coming from the iron pot. It was boiling over. Where was Mama?

Libby looked for her and saw her in the back of the blue wagon.

She ran quickly to the pot. She picked up the long wooden spoon that lay nearby, stuck it into the pot and started to stir as fast as she could. The spoon was big and the fire very hot. She turned her face away to the cool air. As she turned she took a step closer to the fire. Her long skirt brushed against the hot pot and the coals underneath. She smelled something burning. Something touched her legs and spread up to her arms. She batted at it with her hands then looked down to see flames reaching up from the bottom of her skirt. She stamped her feet up and down, batting the hot flames with her hands, then ran screaming toward her mother.

Mama ran quickly to reach Libby. She pushed her to the ground and rolled her in the grass while she beat at the flames with her hands. Finally the flames were gone from Libby's skirt. The bottom was burned black and fell apart in little pieces.Libby lay on the ground sobbing.

Mama wiped her tears away and said, "It's all right now Libby. The fire is out."

Mama cut away Libby's burned skirt and her charred stockings . She gently cleaned the burns on her legs and covered them with Grandma's salve and clean bandages.

Papa came and placed his big hand on top of Libby's head

"I was just trying to help Mama," Libby sobbed.

" I know Libby." Papa said. "I know you were trying to save Mama's stew."

Papa walked away and Libby watched as he went to Mama and helped her bathe her burned hands.

"Abigale, you should put some bandages on those hands," he said.

"Bandages will just get in the way with my work, Caleb," she said. "Grandma's salve will heal them up fine. Nancy will help with the cooking and dishes."

***

Supper was late and the family sat quietly eating the stew that was a little bit burned. Nancy sliced some of Grandma's bread. After supper Libby washed the dishes while she sat on the milk stool and Nancy put things away. Mama and Papa sat by a big tree watching the stars and Will lay by the fire and chewed on a long straw as he looked into the flames and bright coals.

Bedtime came and Mama, Papa and Little Ben slept in the big tent. Libby and Nancy slept in the blue wagon. Will rolled up in his blankets under the freight wagon and Jesse stood the first watch over the cattle and mules until midnight when Will would relieve him.

Libby lay awake listening to the cattle bawling in the distance and to the frogs calling from the stream. She stayed very still to keep her sore legs from hurting and wished that she had not burned herself, her stockings and her good linsey woolsey dress.

Nancy whispered, "I can sew a bottom onto your dress in the morning. Mama has some grey wool that we can use. We can find it in the morning Libby. I expect you will be riding in the wagon for a few days until your legs are better."

Libby felt tears roll down her cheeks. She was nothing but trouble. She tried so hard to do things right but try as much as she could she always seemed to do the wrong thing. She just wanted to help out like everybody else. She wished she could be appreciated like Nancy and Jesse. Even Little Ben was funny and made people laugh.

An owl called from a a nearby tree. Ho-hoo, ho-hoo! Libby wiped her cheeks with her closed fist and pulled her blankets over her head. She lay thinking of Greyboy curled up in a nest of hay in Grandpa's barn loft. She remembered the purring sounds he made when he lay close to her. Soon she was asleep.

***

"Rise and shine", called Jesse and stuck his head into the back of the wagon. A big grin stretched across his face.

Libby looked up at Jesse and then across at Nancy's empty bed and rubbed her sleepy eyes. "Is everybody up all ready?" she asked.

"Yes, and its time for you to rise and shine. Up you come young lady. It's breakfast time."

He picked up Libby in his strong arms and carried her outside and sat her on the milking stool.Nancy brought a tin plate with hot biscuits, bacon and gravy and a cup of cold milk.

After breakfast the wagons were packed and Libby was settled in the family wagon on a soft feather bed. She had her sewing bag with quilt pieces for a nine patch quilt beside her. The big wagon wheels turned and squeaked as they went bumpity bump over the rough places in the road.

Libby tried to keep her feet quiet and her sore legs straight as she worked on her nine patch quilt. She leaned against the side of the wagon and tried to make her stitches tiny as the wagon swayed and jolted. The nine patch block was getting bigger. She had just three pieces left to finish. She laid the quilt block in her lap to wait until the wagon stopped bouncing so much. She wanted Mamma to be proud of her sewing.

The mules' harness jangled, the big wagon wheels rumbled and the cattle bawled from behind. Will cracked his whip in the air to urge the oxen ahead. Libby could feel the hot sun pouring into the back of the wagon. She pulled back her shawl and wiped her face with a cool, damp cloth Mama had left for her. The feather bed seemed flat and hard and Libby wiggled from side to side to try and find a soft spot. Noon time seemed a long time coming but just when she had leaned forward and closed her eyes she heard Papa call.

"Whoa Prince! Whoa Barney!" The big wagon rolled back and forth then stopped.

Libby's head snapped up and she opened her eyes and watched as lunch was spread on the ground in a shady spot under some trees. The family gathered around to eat. Tin plates clanged and Jesse's laughter floated out in the air.

"Everybody go at it. We won't take long for nooning today We have to get on the road soon if we make Independence tonight," Papa said.

Nobody came for Libby. Maybe she would have to help herself, she thought. She reached for the strong bow on the side of the wagon and gripped with both hands. Just as she was about to pull herself up Papa called to her from outside.

"Just a minute young lady. I am coming to lift you out."

Papa placed Libby on the soft grass and Nancy brought her a plate cold beans and bread and a cold cup of water. Libby didn't like beans very much but this time they tasted so good. After the nooning the wagons rolled on through the afternoon. Libby finished her quilt block and folded it carefully placing it in her sewing bag. She watched as the shadows grew longer under the trees along the road. Her head fell forward and she was asleep as the wagon wheels turned round and round and the mules harness jingle, jangled.

"Whoa!" Papa called to the mules and the wagon slowed.

Libby sat up and peeked out the back of the wagon. It was dark outside and all she could see was a thousand twinkling lights in the distance. She leaned out the back of the wagon and listened as Papa and Mama talked about the campfires that twinkled ahead.

"Looks like a lot of folks are gathered here at Independence ready to go west," Papa said.

"Yes, from all the campfires there must be hundreds of people here. Do you suppose we can stop somewhere just this side of all those campfires so we won't get into such a crowd?" Mama asked.

"We'll move on ahead a little way and find a place where we can get water," Papa answered.

The shadows under the trees along the road disappeared as they passed campfire after campfire. Children ran back and forth and dogs barked at them as they passed. They reached a place where a stream ran beside the road. Papa pulled back on the reins and stopped the mules.

"Welcome stranger," a man called out.

A tall, thin man walked over to the wagon and reached his hand toward Papa. "I'm Will Stampers from Tennessee. I am camped just back there a ways. You and yer family headed west?"

"That's right, Mr. Stampers. We are on our way to Oregon territory. This is my wife, Abigale, and these are my children. Have you been camped here long?" Papa asked.

"Six days altogether. The weather has been cold and the

grass along the trail isn't tall enough to feed the livestock so far. I expect we'll have to wait another three, four days fore it grows enough to feed all the cattle that's gonna pass over the trail. We sure hope we don't have to wait much longer."

A small girl with red braids came running up and stood beside Mr. Stampers.

"This here is my daughter, Liza. She must be about the age of your little girl."

"My daughter Libby had an accident and has to sit in the wagon a few days. She would be happy if Liza came over and said hello."

Liza ran over to the back of the wagon and stood on tiptoes looking up at Libby. "Hi. I'm Liza," she said and held out her hand to Libby.

Libby reached down and took Liza's hand and answered, "I'm glad to meet you Liza. I'm Libby. I hope we can be friends. Do you like to sew? I'm making a quilt, a nine patch."

"No, I don't like sewing much. I guess I like to do boy things better than girl things. But we can still be friends can't we?"

"Yes we can. You must help your Mama do girl things some-times don't you?" asked Libby.

"Oh yes. I don't ever get out of dishes and chores. And I like to look for berries and pick wildflowers and Pa made me a doll out of leather. I'll show you."

She ran back toward her family camp calling, "Back in a minute."

Libby opened her sewing bag and unfolded her nine patch quilt block, spreading it over her knee.

"Here she is," called Liza when she came back to the wagon. "Here's Tessie."

She held out a small wooden doll dressed in a buckskin dress and moccasins.

"I'm really too big for dolls but Tessie is special because Pa made her for me. You see, Pa is a carpenter. He can make anything."

"Tessie is a nice doll, Liza. This is my quilt block I just finished." She smoothed her hand across the quilt block on her knee then held it up for Liza to see.

"That's real pretty. Are you going to make a whole quilt all by yourself?" Liza asked.

"Maybe, if I have enough scraps."

"I have to go now," Liza said "I have to wash those pesky

dishes I told you about. I will come see you soon when you get your camp set up."

***

When the tent was set up and a fire built and supper was ready Papa came to the back of the wagon and carried Libby to the milk stool where she sat and ate supper.

"Libby is gonna get to be a lazy bones if she keeps sitting on that stool," Jesse teased.

"I am not," Libby answered. "Mama, I can wash dishes even if I am sitting on a stool can't I?" she asked.

"Yes Libby," Mama answered. "You can help Nancy and then it's bedtime for us all."

"I don't know how much sleep we will get tonight. Seems like noise is coming from every direction. I can hear the clang of anvils, dogs barking and even a few shouts from somebody having trouble. You might want to put your pillow on top of your head tonight instead of of under your head," Papa said and he laughed his big laugh that made his shoulders shake and his head lean back and his lips spread in a big grin.

Long after Libby lay down on her bed and pulled the covers up under her chin she could hear the voices of other campers talking and shouting. Papa was right. It was better to put your pillow over your head and shut out all the noise. She lifted her head, pulled out her pillow, lay it over her head and was soon sound asleep.

JUMPING OFF AT INDEPENDENCE

"Wake up you sleepy head," Liza called from the back of the wagon.

Libby stretched and pushed up on her elbows and looked out the back of the wagon at the bright morning sunshine. Standing right in front of the wagon's pucker hole was Liza.

"My, you sure are an early bird this morning", Libby said.

"Can you get down by yourself? Your Ma is fixing breakfast and you need to get up and eat. We can go explore this camp if you can walk," Liza said.

Libby pushed herself up and stood for a moment, She reached for her dress then stood looking at Liza.

"Oh, all right. We are both girls but I get it. You don't want me to see you take off your nightgown. I'll just turn my back to you and I won't see a thing."

Libby tested her sore legs and took a step. Everything seemed fine so she quickly dressed, then made her hair neat with her hair brush.

The girls hurried over to the breakfast campfire and Nancy

handed Libby a bowl of cornmeal mush covered with milk and sugar.

“Would you like a bowl?" Nancy asked Liza.

"Oh, no ma’am. I had my breakfast real early. My Pa is checking out the grass this morning and he wanted to get an early start. He is going across the river to take a look. He says the grass has to be tall enough to feed the cattle and horses before we can start across the prairie.”

Libby finished her mush and rinsed out her bowl and spoon then carefully put them away in the grub box and walked over to the big tent where her mother was folding blankets.

"Good morning Libby. I am glad to see you are up walking this morning. Are your legs feeling better?" she asked.

"A lot better, Mama,” Libby answered. “Could I take a walk around camp with Liza?"

"As long as you don't go too far. Make sure you know your way back to our wagon. There are a lot of people camped here and it would be easy to lose your way.”

The two girls held hands and walked down a dirt road. There were wagons all along the road where families had made camp. Children ran in and out of the camps playing tag and running out to stare at Libby and Liza. Dogs barked and strained to get loose from their leashes when the girls walked by. They walked past a man shoeing horses and another pounding a wagon wheel rim on an anvil.

"Where are we going, Liza?" Libby asked.

"Oh, just down this road a little farther. There is a tin peddler's wagon up this way and we can see what he has for sale."

" I don't have money to buy anything from a peddler Liza," Libby answered.

"Oh, I don't either. It 's fun just the same to watch him pull out all the boxes and drawers to show what's inside."

They walked down the road until they reached a small hill where a peddler's wagon sat at the top. The wagon was painted red with rows of drawers on the sides and lanterns and pails hanging on it.

The girls reached the top of the hill and walked up. A small, brown man with a bright red kerchief, brown baggy pants and a dull, yellow shirt came toward them.

"Well, young ladies, what can I help you with this fine morning? How about a bright tin cup or a pretty pitcher for your mama? I have pans and buckets, plates and cups and everything you might need on your trip to Or-a-gone."

"Oh no, Mister Murphy. My friend Libby and I just want to look at your wares," Liza answered.

"Well, now. I have some fine things today. Just look at these whirly-gigs," he said and pulled open a drawer with shinny pin wheels. He picked up one and let the wind catch it, sending the wheel whirling around and around.

Liza and Libby stood watching, eyes wide as they looked at the shinny wheel turn in the wind.

"That is a beauty all right Mister Murphy but I can't buy anything today. We just wanted to have a look," said Liza.

"Well then, until the next time you come by Miss Liza. Tell your mama I got a dishpan for her if she needs one."

"I will Mr. Murphy, said Liza. "Goodby."

The girls walked down the hill and just as they reached the bottom, a giant dog came charging toward them in a whirl of dust and black fur. His open mouth showed sharp teeth and a fierce growl came from his throat.

"Run Libby. Run for your life," Liza shouted.

The girls ran across the road away from the growling dog. They ran past wagons and people around their campfires. They ran past a blacksmith shoeing a mule. Libby knocked over a tin bucket which rolled in front of the skittish mule causing him to jerk away from the angry blacksmith who shook his fist at the girls and shouted. "Get goin, you rascals."

"Hurry Libby," Liza urged as she went went flying away, kicking up dust as she ran.

Libby struggled to keep up but her legs felt stiff and sore and she limped along slowly trying to catch Liza. When Liza was almost out of sight. Libby called. "Liza. Stop. Wait for me."

Liza turned and ran back to Libby.

"That old dog is gone now Libby."

She looked at Libby's tear streaked face and then saw the bandage that had come loose and fallen down around the tops of Libby's shoes.

"Oh, Libby. Your sore legs are really troublesome. Come on. We have to get back to camp so your Mama can fix them." She reached for Libby's hand and the girls walked slowly down the road.

They passed family camps and curious children who stared at them. One big boy was leaning against a wagon, his hands in his pockets, and an angry frown on his face.

He called, "Where do you two little bag-o-bones think you

are goin?"

Liza tightened her grip on Libby's hand and pulled her ahead.

The girls met some boys driving cattle and Liza guided Libby over to a giant tree. They stood behind the tree and waited for them pass.

"Liza, please," begged Libby. " I just have to sit down and rest."

"Yes, I guess you are gettin tuckered out with your sore legs." said Liza. "It must be past noon by now. I think we have missed our nooning meal but I don't know which way is home. We have passed so many camps. Let's go up to that grove of trees and maybe we can rest for awhile."

When the girls reached the trees Libby lay down on some soft grass. Lizzie carefully lifted Libby's skirt and looked at her sore legs. "You are hurtin for sure Libby. I'm gonna wrap the bandages back on your legs so they won't be rubbed by your skirt tail."

Liza wound the cloth around Libby's sore legs and said, "There, that ought to help some Libby,"

Liza rested her back against a tree trunk and gently touched Libby's shoulder."Libby," she said, "rest your head in my lap and stretch out your sore legs. When you are able we'll head out toward camp if we can figure out which way to go."

The tired girls closed their eyes and were soon asleep. The sun sank low toward the tree tops, shadows darkened under the trees, and the crickets began their evening song. Libby and Liza slept soundly as the afternoon turned to evening. Men were shouting in the distance and cows mooed for their young calves. There was pounding and banging from men fixing wagon wheels and children's shrill voices came from camps all around. The exhausted girls slept on.

***

It was almost dark when something awakened Libby. She sat up and stared out from the dusky grove. The shadows under the trees were black now and she could not see anything there. Only the white tops of wagons showed up in the dark.

Then she heard it. It was Maggie's whinny. Somewhere Jesse was riding her. Libby stood up and hurried out from under the trees looking into the darkness. She could see a shadow moving closer. It was Jesse on Maggie.

She waved her arms calling, "Jesse, Jesse. We're over here. Over here."

The black mare came speeding toward the grove with her rider bent over the saddle urging her on. When they reached the grove Jesse pulled back on the reins, stopping the mare in a flurry of prancing hoofs and a cloud of dust.

"Libby, thank goodness I found you. We have all been out looking for you. Where is Liza? Her Pa is awfully worried about her," Jesse said.

"I'm right here. Right here with Libby. We want to get home. Can you take us Jesse?" Liza asked.

"Mount up behind me Liza and wrap your arms around my waist and hang on tight. You can ride in front of me, Libby," said Jesse and he reached down with his outstretched arm to help the girls up onto Maggie's back.

"Ye-haw, Maggie." Jesse called and urged Maggie back toward the home camp.

When Jesse rode into camp with the two girls, Liza's Pa reached up and lifted her down.
"Young lady, you have some explaining to do. I have told you before not to go so far as that peddler wagon."

He gripped Liza's arm and moved so fast toward their camp that her feet almost flew off the ground. Jesse carefully lifted Libby down from the front of the saddle then led Maggie away for feed and water. Mama and Papa were standing silently beside the family wagon.

" We were very worried about you, Libby," Mama said. "We have been looking for you most of the day and Papa has not been able to get ready to cross the river. I think you should be sorry to cause your family so much worry and trouble."

"My daughter," Papa said. "If those sore legs haven't punished you enough I think I can find something else that will help you remember to think for yourself and not follow Liza or anyone else who isn't using good judgment. From today on you are to ask for your parents' permission to leave our camp for any reason. Let there be no excuse for you to forget to do so. I am disappointed in you Libby," Papa said and he bent his head down toward his chest and closed his tired eyes while his shoulders slumped forward.

"Papa," Libby said softly, "I'm awfully sorry," and she touched her Papa gently on his shoulder.

Papa turned to her and smiled. "I know you are Libby. Now go and get your sore legs attended to."

Libby walked slowly. Her stiff legs refused to move fast as she went around the wagon to find Mamma. When her legs were cleaned, treated with salve and bandaged with clean bandages, she rested on her bed in the wagon. Nancy brought her some stew and and without saying anything at all, wrapped her arms around Libby's shoulders and gave her a warm hug.

When Nancy had gone Libby wondered why she had followed Liza to the peddler wagon? Why didn't they come back sooner? She should have said no but she just followed after Liza. Could she ever do anything right?

"I'm just trouble all the time," she whispered into the dark and tears wet her cheeks. She had to rub them dry with the sleeve of her nightgown.

She lay quietly in the wagon listening to the sounds of the camp. When everyone had gone to bed and Nancy had come to her bed and the camp was quiet, Libby lay thinking of her long, terrible day. Tomorrow she would do better. She would think for herself.

CROSSING THE MISSOURI

The morning sun was bright as it streamed into the back of the wagon. Libby could hear loud noises coming from everywhere. She sat up and slowly and lifted her legs over the bedside. She pushed herself up and stood, testing her legs.

"Ouch," she said as she felt the strain on her sore legs. "I can do this."

She moved over to get her dress and tidy herself. She climbed down from the wagon then went to find Mama and Nancy at the campfire.

"Good morning Libby," Mama said. "How are your legs feeling?"

"I can walk on them Mama and I am going to help you all I can. If you will tell me something to do I am going to try to do it right."

"All right, Libby. Get Ben and make sure his face and hands are clean for breakfast. Papa and Jesse are doing chores and will be back soon."

When Papa and Jesse sat down for breakfast, Papa told them Will had gone with Mr. Stampers to check on a ferry that would take them across the Missouri river.

"We are hoping to get in line for the ferry tomorrow morning. Mr. Stampers says he was over the river yesterday and the grass is high enough to feed the livestock on the trail. Tonight we will meet with some of the folks that are ready to go and choose a captain. Will says there is a scout named Redtop that will guide us for the right pay. He was a scout for Will's last pack trip and Will says he knows the territory."

After supper Papa went to a meeting to find out who was going to be in the wagon train and who would be captain and guide.

Mama, Nancy and Libby sat around the campfire watching the red flames grow smaller until only bright coals glowed in the dark. It grew late as they waited up for Papa. The stars came out and the big yellow moon spread light around the campfire. Finally, they heard footsteps and Papa came walking out of the darkness.

He sat down next to Mama and said, "Well, we are all set to leave tomorrow morning. Albert Jamison will be the captain. From Illinois. He seems to be a good man. We have hired Redtop for scout. Each of the thirty families going in the train pays for part of his services. I think we have a good group."

"Will the Stampers family be going with us?" Mama asked.

"Yes, they are going in our group and Libby, Liza may get a little adventurous on the trail but I expect you to keep your wits about you."

"Can I still play with Liza, Papa?," Libby asked.

"Yes, you can play with Liza but instead of following her lead all the time, do your own thinking. Now, time for bed. We must have the wagons on the road by day break."

Later that night, Libby pulled the covers up to her chin. She lay in bed listening to the sounds around their camp. Dogs barked, voices called from far away and Nancy's soft breathing came from her bed across from Libby's. Tomorrow there would be a lot of excitement. They were going to cross the big, wide Missouri river. She turned her face toward the wagon cover and closed her eyes to sleep.

***

It was still dark next morning when sounds came from outside the wagon. Mama was fixing breakfast and Nancy had all ready gone to help. Libby scrambled out of bed, quickly dressed, and brushed back the loose curls that had fallen from her braids. She climbed down from the wagon and found her family gathered around the fire with their bowls of cornmeal mush and bacon and bread. Nancy handed Libby a bowl of mush and a biscuit with a piece of bacon inside. The family ate with little talk. They were all thinking about crossing the wide and dangerous Missouri River.

"Let's get everything packed," Papa said. "The sun will soon be up and it will be time for us to join the others at the landing to wait for our turn to cross on the ferry."

Everything was made ready and Papa and Will hitched the teams to the wagons. The family climbed into the family wagon and Papa called to the mules.

"Ho! Get up there."

The big blue wagon rolled ahead with Will and the ox team. Jesse and Maggie driving the cattle followed behind. When Libby looked out the back of the wagon she could see Liza waving from the Stamper wagon. Libby stood up and waved her sunbonnet to let Liza know that she saw her.

When they got close to the ferry crossing there were wagons lined up from the river for a very long way . There were wagons on the right and wagons on the left. Wagons reached up the middle of the bank as far as you could see.

Papa drove the mules to a place in line behind the last wagon on the right side. The wagon eased down slowly as the line in front moved ahead. Will pulled the ox wagon in behind the family wagon and slowly followed the line toward the river.

When they reached the landing Papa got a ride on a ferry just leaving to cross the river. The oxen and mules were unhitched from the wagons and their oxbows and harness put in the freight wagon. Will and Jesse drove the animals down to the water's edge. They shouted and pushed until they plunged into the deep river. Jesse took off Maggie's saddle and bridle, patted Maggie on the neck, and talked to her softly. He then smacked her on the shoulder and she jumped into the river. Will and Jesse then moved the cattle to the river bank and pushed them ahead until they plunged in behind.

Papa stood waiting on the far side of the river. He watched as the big waves rolled over the cattle's backs and pushed against them. They swam to the opposite bank and scrambled up out of the water. Papa ran down along the edge of the river and got hold of the mules and Maggie as they climbed out of the water. The big, lumbering oxen moved slowly across the river, and reaching the far bank, stood waiting patiently.

The ferrymen started the ferry with the two loaded wagons. Libby stood at the back of the wagon holding on to Ben's hand. Mama and Nancy stood in the front of the wagon holding on to the seat. Will and Jesse stood on the ferry floor behind the wagons.

As Libby looked out at the deep, dark water a sudden gust of wind blew a giant wave up over the edge of the ferry, flooding the deck with water and sending the ferry sideways. Libby screamed and climbed up on top of a trunk that was stacked on top of some barrels. She reached down to pull Ben up and suddenly the trunk rolled down, turning over a barrel of corn meal.

The ferry danced up and down and the ferrymens' loud voices rang out. They quickly sprang to the side and dipped their paddles up and down faster and faster in the water until the ferry turned and faced the far riverbank. Slowly they moved across the water until at last, they reached the bank. The mules and oxen were hitched to the wagons and pulled them through the mud and sand away from the river and up to the grassy prairie.

Papa shouted, "Is everybody safe?"

Libby sat on on the floor of the wagon, right in the middle of the spilled corn meal and covered her face with her hands. She had caused the barrel to fall over. She sat very still waiting to see what Papa would say.

Papa stuck his head inside the wagon's pucker hole and asked, "What has happened here? How did that barrel get overturned?"

"Papa," Nancy answered, "Libby got scared and climbed up on the trunk that was on top of the barrel. The trunk came tumbling down and knocked over the barrel. "

"Libby!" Papa shouted. "Do you know that meal was for

our entire trip?"

"I was scared of the water," she said as she folded her arms over her face to hide her tears.

"All right Libby. This is going to be a long and dangerous journey and you can't afford to be afraid all the time." Papa said and swung away from the wagon.

Mama and Nancy helped Libby scoop up the meal that was spilled and sift out the sticks and leaves. They pushed and shoved until the barrel stood upright again and the spilled meal was put back inside the barrel. Mama put its cover on and made sure it was fastened in place then, with Nancy's help, she and Nancy put her trunk back on top.

"This lid should have been on the barrel in the first place. If had been tight the meal wouldn't have spilled. I'm sorry you were so afraid, Libby". She put her arms around Libby and hugged her.

The wagons moved ahead over mud and deep ruts and on to the grassy prairie. Libby looked out the back of the family wagon. The green grass rolled in waves across the prairie as far as she could see. She watched the red sky as the giant sun moved down toward the horizon. Shadows crept out from under the wagon. The mules pulled them off the trail and over the grass. Papa pulled back on the reins and called "Woah!"

Libby climbed down from the wagon and watched as other wagons followed, pulling up to make one big circle with an opening on one side. The horses and oxen were unhitched and taken to a stream for water. A fire pit was dug and Mama set up the the cooking pot.

"Libby", Mama said, "watch Ben while I am cooking supper."

"Yes, I will Mama,"Libby answered. She walked around the wagon and found Ben watching as Will greased the wagon axles.

"Is Ben helping you, Will?" Libby asked.

"More watchin than helpin I'de say," Will said.

"I'll make sure he doesn't get in the way Will," Libby said.

Will turned and hung the grease bucket back on the wagon. "Peers like this job is done for the day," he said, "but these wheels will need a good greasin agin tomorrow and I don't care if Ben wants to watch. The little feller needs to learn things. Someday he can take over this job."

"I could learn to grease wheels, Will," Libby said.

"Nah, this ain't no job for girls. You better go help your

Mama fix the supper. I shore am hungry."

Libby took Ben's hand and walked back to the cooking fire. "Ben," she said. "sit right here and watch Mama fry the bacon. She has cornbread baking in the dutch oven too. I can get out the tin plates and cups to help her.

She found dishes in the grub box and set them on the the quilt spread on the ground. Mama looked up from the cooking fire and brushed the smoke away from her face. She took the hot skillet with the frying bacon and set it on the ground beside the fire.

"Libby, find your Papa. Supper is ready."

Libby took Ben's hand and hurried around the wagon to find Papa, Will and Jesse.

"Supper," called Libby.

Everyone came quickly to the fire.

"I'm hungry as a bear," Jesse said and hurried to fill his plate.

While the family was sitting on the ground near the campfire eating supper, Mr. Stampers and Liza walked up to join them.

"Good evening folks," Mr. Stampers said. Liza, who stood behind him, giggled and covered her face with her hands.

"Sit down and join us, Stampers," Papa said.

"Don't mind if I do," Mr. Stampers replied and sat down on the grass beside Papa.

Liza hurried over to sit beside Libby. "Look Libby. I brought my doll, Tessie, with me. We can play with her. Let's take her over to that log by the river and play house."

"Mama, may I go play with Liza?" Libby asked.

"Yes, if you will carry a bucket of water for dish washing," Mama answered.

"Come on Libby. Get your bucket and let's go," Liza said and jumped up and ran with Libby to the wagon to get a water bucket.

They hurried to the river, filled the bucket, splashing water over the sides all the way back to the campfire.

"Here it is Mama," Libby said. "We are going back to the big log by the river."

The girls hurried back to the big log, cleaned away old leaves, and used a brush broom to sweep the log clean. Liza picked leaves from a low hanging branch of a cottonwood tree then spread them out on the log for a blanket for Tessie. She gently lay Tessie on the leaves and covered her with a small handkerchief she pulled from her apron pocket.

"Let's sit down by the log and be be quiet so Tessie can fall asleep," said Liza.

"I can't hear anything but crickets chirping," said Libby.

"I know," said Liza. "But we still need to be as quiet as we can because Tessie will not go to sleep if we talk."

"Oh, Tessie is just a doll Liza. She can't hear anything."

"I know she's a doll but I pretend she's real cause I don't have anybody else to talk to. Mama and Papa work all the time. So it's just me and Tessie."

"Well, I have lots of people in my family but do you know what? They don't talk a lot to me. I don't seem to fit in any-place," said Libby.

"Oh, you will, Libby. You'll get some attention one of these days when you do something big and spectacular."

"Do you really think so, Liza? "

"For sure, Libby. It will happen. You just wait and see. Shush now and let Tessie sleep."

The girls sat by the log listening to the insects singing in the evening air. They lowered their heads against the log and were soon dozing.

The snap of a twig startled Libby and she jumped up and saw a tall Indian dressed in buckskin standing just behind them and beside him was a small girl in a long buckskin dress and moccasins.

Libby screamed,"Indians!"

Liza jumped up beside her and the girls ran as fast as their feet would fly to the campfire.

" Indians, Indians," sobbed Libby.

"They are right back of that log," said Liza pointing in that direction.

The men ran to the wagons for their guns and the women and children quickly ran to take cover inside the wagons. Libby sat inside the family wagon with Mama, Nancy and Ben. She felt her heart pounding as she listened to the shouts of the men as they ran past the wagon to the river.

Jesse and Papa were gone a long time then Libby heard Papa shout, "They're gone boys. But they may be back later."

Jesse and Papa looked into the back of the wagon and Papa

said, "They have gone. We saw the moccasin prints down by the river but they were nowhere to be seen."

"Maybe they didn't mean any harm," Mama said.

"That may be," Papa answered, "but we can't take a chance. Captain Jamison will post a double guard. I will be on first watch tonight along with Jesse. Will Stampers and Redtop will relieve us."

In the dark Libby lay in her bed listening to every sound outside the wagon. "Nancy, are you awake?" she whispered.

"Hush Libby. It's best if we keep still. Papa and Jesse are out there watching for us and we can help them best by keeping quiet. Now go to sleep. We are safe for now."

In the early light Libby sat up in her bed. People were getting up and moving about. She climbed across her bed and looked out back. There was Jesse rolled up in his blanket sleeping under the wagon. He was back from his time at watch. She hurried to get dressed. Nancy was up too and the girls climbed down from the wagon. There outside stood Liza.

She came over to Libby and sobbed, "My Tessie is gone, Libby. I left her on the log when we ran from the Indians and when I looked for her this morning she was gone."

“I am so sorry Liza”, said Libby. “I wonder if the Indians took her. Maybe that Indian girl wanted her.”

Nancy wiped Liza’s cheeks with the palms of her hands and smoothed her curly hair away from her face. “Don’t cry, Liza,” she said. “I know you loved your doll but maybe I can make you a rag doll out of scraps I have in my quilt bag. It won’t be the same as Tessie but it will be a new doll and you can give her a special name. One you find on the way to Oregon.”

Liza sniffed and held back her sobs and smiled. “Would you do that for me Nancy?” she asked.

“I will get started on it today,” Nancy answered.

Liza turned and ran back toward her family wagon.

“Nancy, ” Libby said, “it will be nice if you make Liza a doll. I should have helped her remember to get Tessie but we were so afraid of the Indians.”

“The Indians are gone now so let’s go help Mama with breakfast. It will be time to roll out soon,” Nancy said.

***

Bumpity, bump, bump. The wagon wheels went up and down out of the the holes and over the mounds of dirt on the trail. Nancy and Libby sat inside the wagon on their beds sewing Liza's rag doll.

"I think she would like this blue for a dress," said Libby.

"Most likely she would," answered Nancy, "but first we have to finish the body. I have stitched the arms, legs, and body together. You can fill them with some soft scraps from this old dish towel. If you cut it up in small pieces it will work just fine for stuffing. "

The girls worked quietly until the sun shone into the opening of the wagon cover making the wagon hot. Libby pulled on the pucker string and loosened it to make the opening bigger. A breeze came through the back of the wagon and the two girls stood up letting the cool air blow through their hair.

"Hold on Libby. This wagon is a bumpy ride. We don't want to tumble out the back. "

"Liza says she can jump from the wagon while it is still moving. It's no trouble at all she says."

"Better do your own thinking, Libby, just like Papa said. Liza should wait until the wagon stops." Nancy grabbed a wagon bow as the wagon wheel on her side of the wagon went up over a bush.

"See, just like that you can lose your balance and fall out of the wagon, maybe under the wheel."

"I think I'll wait for Papa to stop the mules before I get out. Now that the doll's body is almost finished, do you think we can work on the clothes tonight?"

"We should be able to after supper. You can embroider a face. I have some colored thread in my bag. You will need some red for lips and black for eyes. We can find a few scraps of yarn and make some hair."

"Whoa!" Papa called to the mules and the wagon stopped.

"Time for nooning," he said. He unhitched the mules and drove them to the river for a drink.

"Get the dishes out of the grub box girls and we will have a cold meal this noon. There won't be time to make a fire for cooking. " Mama said.

Mama set out a black iron pot of beans and Nancy cut up pieces of cornbread. Libby set out a tin bucket of molasses.

Get some water Libby. Find a shallow place at the edge of the river. It will be muddy but we can let it set for awhile to settle.

Libby walked with a water pail to the edge of the wide Platte River. She followed a path that led to the water's edge. It looked muddy around the path as if animals had walked there for water. She moved upstream to a little pool of deep water and leaned over and dipped in the bucket then reached with both hands to lift the full pail, sloshing some on her skirt as she brought it up.

"Oh, shucks!" she said but smiled as the cool skirt brushed her legs.

She struggled with the heavy pail along the river's edge, listening to the birds in the cottonwood trees noisily pecking at the flies that buzzed around the river. She hurried across the dusty path to the the camp and set the water down on the grub box.

"My, that water is too muddy to clear anytime soon. Best we go ahead and finish our meal and by that time we can use it," Mama said.

Jesse walked over to the bucket of water, hot and thirsty from herding the cattle. He looked at the muddy water and shook his head.

"Bet you can't run fast enough to get away from a cool dash of water Libby, " he said, and put the dipper into the water bucket, then sent water flying to catch the top of Libby's head. Libby ran away screaming. She turned, wiping her face with both hands as the water ran down her cheeks.

"I'll get you Jesse, " she shouted, and went flying toward Jesse who stood by the water bucket shaking with laughter. Just as she reached out toward Jesse she stumbled over a bush and went flying into the water bucket sending it rolling across the ground, the water spilling over her as she fell.She lay on the ground covered with water and dirt.

"Well, don't just stay there mad as a hornet," Jesse said, laughing louder than ever.

To make Libby even more angry, Papa, Mama, Nancy and even Ben laughed too.

Jesse reached down his hand to help Libby up but she jerked her arm away, stumbled up and ran back to the river. She sat under a cottonwood tree, her back against its firm trunk. Grasping her knees she leaned her head forward resting it on her knees and sobbed. She wondered why her family had laughed at her. It wasn't her fault. It was Jesse who threw the water. Why does everybody love Jesse and nobody likes me she wondered? It wasn't fair. She didn't want to go back to the wagon. Maybe they won't even miss me and then when they do they will be sorry.

***

Shouts came from the camp as the wagon train got ready to move on. Libby stirred and lifted her head and slapped at the stubborn mosquitoes that nipped at her face. She looked down the path and saw Nancy coming toward her. She scrunched up tighter trying to make herself as small as possible. Maybe Nancy wouldn't see her. But Nancy came straight to her and bent down beside her. As Libby squeezed her eyes closed she felt Nancy's arms reach around her shoulders and hold her tight.

"I am sorry you got so wet and dirty Libby. I brought the water bucket and we can fill it with water and give you a shower." said Nancy.

"I don't care about getting dirty," said Libby. "I just don't like to be laughed at like it was my fault," she sobbed.

"We didn't laugh at you, Libby. We were laughing at that silly old bucket rolling around in the dirt. Jesse was tired and thirsty and saw the water was too muddy to drink so he wanted to have a little fun. He didn't mean to make fun of you."

"But it seemed like you were all laughing at me." Libby said and stopped her sobbing.

"Here," said Nancy, "Use this big cottonwood leaf for a hankie and blow your nose," and she handed Libby a big green leaf.

Libby stood up, blew her nose, and wiped at her muddy cheeks. The girls walked to the river and filled the water bucket. Nancy poured water over Libby's head letting it run down her cheeks, across her shoulders and down over her skirt. The mud puddled around her bare feet until she stepped onto a patch of green grass and stood, letting the water run from her dripping clothes.

"The sun will dry you out pretty quickly Libby, so let's get back to the wagon before the train starts moving out," said Nancy.

When they reached the wagon Papa was hitching up the mules.

"Ready to go, girls?" he asked.

"We are ready Papa, " Nancy answered. "

They walked beside the family wagon. Libby's wet skirt clung to her legs as she walked but the sun soon dried it. She looked for wildflowers and found white and purple daisies and blue larkspurs. She filled her apron with them.

BUFFALO HUNT

Captain Jamison called out, " Hoah!"

Papa pulled on the reins and stopped the mules.

"Must be some trouble ahead." Papa said.

Mr. Stampers came running from his wagon shouting. Buffalo coming. They are headin down to the river for water. Better not get in their way. Hear that rumble? If you look up yonder at that knoll you can see that black cloud swarmin down. You can feel the ground shakin too. I aim to grab my rifle and see if I can get one of them beggars an if I'm lucky we'll have fresh meat for supper. If they head this way get in the wagons They can be mean critters."

Libby watched as Papa reached for his and Jesse's rifles and ran to meet Jesse. He handed Jesse his rifle, then Jesse got on Maggie and raced toward the buffalo herd that was now crossing the trail in front of the wagons.

As riders swooped down beside the buffalo, a large bull spun away from the herd and headed their way. His giant, shaggy head reached down toward the ground and he kicked up puffs of dust as he ran toward the mules. Toby and Tucker, the lead mules, reared up filling the air with their screams. The other mules, Prince and Barney, pushed back against the wagon keeping it from moving forward.

Mr. Stampers rushed up with his rifle and took aim as the buffalo bull ran around the wagon. The mules plunged, moving the wagon from side to side, almost turning it over before Nancy and Mama got hold of the lead mules' bridles pulling them down talking softly to them. Mr Stampers ran after the big shaggy beast, and before it could run into the trees along the river, he fired his rifle once, then twice, and the big buffalo fell to the ground.

Liza and Libby ran toward the buffalo but Mr Stampers yelled, " hold on there girls. This buffalo may not be done for yet. Don't get too close. He might come charging up again."

The girls stopped and stood watching and listening as shouts and rifle shots came from the men on horseback following the buffalo.

Jesse came riding back on Maggie with his rifle across his saddle. "I got one Papa," he shouted. It's back there in that little draw. Can you help me bring it in?"

"Let's go get it, son,"

The wagons circled close to the river for the night. There

would be no more traveling for the day. There was meat to prepare before dark Mama fried buffalo steaks for supper. Libby had never tasted such a good supper. There was steak with gravy, cornbread and beans and wild strawberries with cream.

spread the big buffalo hide out on the ground. It was soft and curly on one side and Papa said it would make Jesse a fine buffalo robe when it was cured.

"I guess I won't get cold in Oregon this winter," Jesse said.

Nancy and Libby did the dishes. When everything was put away Liza and Mr. Stampers came over to their campfire with his fiddle and he started playing. Soon other people came close to the fire.

Jesse, still in high spirits from the excitement of the buffalo hunt yelled, " Let's honor your partner and dance."

Couples gathered in a square and Liza and Libby sat down on an oxbow to watch.

A tall, young man with dark hair and eyes wearing a faded blue shirt walked up to Nancy and said, "May I have this dance my lady?"

Libby's mouth flew open in surprise. Who was this man anyway? He didn't know her big sister. What right did he have asking her to dance? She hadn't even seen him before.

"Nancy sure won't dance with him, Liza. She doesn't accept dances with strangers," Libby said anxiously.

Before she had finished speaking, the young man swept off his dusty black hat and held it behind his back as he bent at the waist and bowed to her sister.

"Well, sir," answered Nancy. " and who might be asking me for a dance?"

"Oh, I am sorry. I know who you are so I just supposed….but then because I know you are Nancy Campbell and the prettiest girl in this wagon train doesn't mean you know me. I'm Mason Connors. I am with my Pa Justin Connors, my Ma Matilda, and two little sisters Becky and Lydia. Our wagon is about four wagons back.

"Well, Mr. Connors, I am happy to make your acquaintance. I don't usually dance with young men I don't know but since this has been an extraordinary day I'll dance with you this once," Nancy answered.

Liza put her hands over her mouth and giggled and Libby stood up, put her hands on her hips, stomped her foot and said, "Wait til Mama sees this."

Mr. Stampers happily called out "What better time to have

a little Buffalo Gals?" He drew his bow across his fiddle and nearby, a guitar and a banjo joined in. The music filled the night air, reaching across the wide prairie, and up toward the bright stars that covered the endless sky.

Will walked up to the fire and Jesse shouted, "Call this dance for us, Will."

Will stepped closer to the musicians and shouted, "Lets make the calico crack, boys."

Honor your partner.

All join hands and circle to the left.

Fall back in a single line, ladies in front and gents behind.

Swing your partner, corner too.

Right and left all the way through."

Skirts flew and boots stomped as the dancers moved over the ground. Libby and Liza clapped in time to the music along with everyone gathered around the fire. Laughter floated through the dark night as the dancers spun and skipped to the music. Papa put a log on the fire and a shower of sparks flew up into the air with a snap and crackle.

Liza pulled on Libby's hand. "Come on Libby. We can

dance too. We can dance right here."

She pulled Libby up and grabbing her around the waist, spun her around making their feet fly. Around and around in time to the music they spun, until the music stopped and the dancers shuffled back to the fire, huffing and puffing for an extra breath of cool, night air. Laughter swept around the campfire as the ladies sat down to take a needed rest.

Nancy came over to sit with Liza and Libby.

"Liza looked up into Nancy's flushed face and asked, "You got a beau Nancy?"

"No, Liza, I don't have a beau."

"Well, we sure saw you dancin with somebody, didn't we, Libby?

"Yes, and you don't even know that man, Nancy," said Libby. "What's Mama gonna think when she finds out you accepted a dance from a stranger?"

"Libby," Nancy asked, "Are you planning on telling Mama?"

"I am because Mama has always said don't accept invitations from people you don't know and I'm going to tell her right now."

She turned around and ran to the family wagon without waiting to hear what Nancy was calling to her.Mama looked surprised as Libby climbed into the back of the wagon.

"Libby, I thought you were with Liza at the dance. Are you all right?"

"I am Mama. Did you put Ben to sleep?"

" He's asleep in the tent. He was just too tired to stay awake any longer. But why did you leave Liza and the dance?"

"Mama, something bad happened. Something you won't like and it's about Nancy. This man came up and asked her to dance and he was a perfect stranger. And do you know what? Nancy took his hand and went off and danced with him."

"Well, did he say who he was and where he came from?" asked Mama.

"He said his name was Mason Connors. I know Nancy didn't know him but he sweet talked her into dancing with him. He said she was the prettiest girl in the train and that he and his mama and papa and two sisters were in this wagon train about four wagons back."

"Now Libby, your sister is growing up. Some day she will marry and leave home. You will not always be able to have so much attention from her. She will want to have a family of her own and she will leave our home and you will be the young lady of the house."

"But Mama, you always said not to be familiar with strangers. Nancy didn't know that man and she danced with him." Libby insisted.

"This journey puts a different light on a lot of things. We are no longer in our home community and we must judge things from our own heart and observations. In one sense all the people in the wagon train are one community. We are all trying to accomplish the same thing, reach Oregon."

"You mean it's all right to talk to strangers?" asked Libby.

"You must remember to watch people's behavior and judge them by their actions."

"Well I don't think I like him anyway."

"I think your sister is a wise young woman and I don't think she will take up with anyone that isn't a good man. Don't be jealous of your sister's friends, Libby. It will not take away from her love for you. Nancy has a big heart with room for more than one in it."

"I guess so," sniffed Libby, thinking of the feel of her sister's warm hugs and the sound of her happy laughter. Would there be any more good times making rag dolls and picking wildflowers?

"I think I will just stay here with you Mama. I don't feel much like dancing anymore."

Libby sat quietly on her bed listening to the sounds from outside the wagon. The music was playing again and in spite of her glum face and pouting lips she found herself tapping her feet in time to the music.

"The music sounds good doesn't it Libby?" Mama asked. "Makes a body want to move your feet all right. If you will watch Ben in the tent, I think I will walk over and dance with your Papa."

"I'll watch him, Mama," Libby agreed. In some way she had disappointed Mama. She could tell. She wanted to make Mama happy with her again.

"I'll go sit in the tent so I can keep a close eye on him Mama," she said.

"That's good Libby, " Mama said and put her arm across Libby's shoulders and gave her a hug. "I won't be gone long and then you can come back into the wagon for the night."

Libby sat on the end of Ben's pallet and curled her arms

around her bent knees. She could hear the music and Will's dance calls and the laughter and shouts of the people around the camp fire. She lay her head on her knees. She felt a tear slip down her cheek. She was sure she was right but Mama seemed disappointed with her and now Nancy would be angry with her too for telling Mama about her and the stranger. She lay down beside Ben and was soon sleep.

***

"Wake up, Libby. Time to go to your bed."

In the dim lantern light, Libby looked up into Mama's smiling face and reached up to take her hand and pulled herself up from Ben's bed.

"I guess I fell asleep", she said.

"Yes, now go on to the wagon. Nancy is there now. See you in the morning."

Libby hurried to the wagon and quickly dressed in her nightgown and lay down on her bed. "Nancy," she called softly. "Are you asleep?"

"No, not yet, Libby", she answered.

"Did you have a good time dancing with that man?"

"I did Libby and he isn't that man. His name is Mason

Connors," Nancy answered.

"I know, but you didn't know him until tonight," Libby said.

"I know him now and he is a nice man. I can tell."

"I'm sorry I ran off and told Mama. You probably wanted to tell her yourself," Libby said and a small sob escaped as her shoulders shook.

"Don't worry Libby. You will always be my number one sister. Nothing will ever change that. Tomorrow we will finish Liza's doll and give it to her. Good night little sister."

"Nite Nancy," Libby answered softly.

For a long time Libby lay listening to the night sounds. A wolf howled from far away and a dog in the camp answered back with his own lonesome reply. Tomorrow she would try to think of other people's feelings. She would be especially nice to Mama and Nancy who still loved her even when she was a tattletale.

Morning light came in around the pucker strings of the wagon cover. In the dim light Libby could see that Nancy was still sleeping. She quietly dressed and hurried outside to the cooking fire where Mama was fixing breakfast.

"Morning Libby." she said.

"Morning, Mama. Can I help with breakfast?"

"Please go and wake Nancy. It seems she is extra tired after the dancing last night."

"I'll get her Mama and I won't say a word about her dancing with a stranger."

"Best not Libby. Best to let your sister do her own telling."

Libby poked her head inside the wagon and saw Nancy brushing her long dark hair. "Are you ready for breakfast Nancy?"

"Oh dear, Libby. I overslept. It will soon be time for the wagons to pull out and I need to help Mama put things away."

The Johnny Cake and bacon was finished and the last of the coffee was gone. Dishes were packed, the water barrel filled, the tent folded, and dust shook out of the blankets.

"Wagons Hoo-ah!" called Captain Jamison.

The Campbell family waited until the other wagons moved out ahead. Today was their day to travel last in line.

***

"The dust is truly pesky," Libby said as she walked beside Nancy next to their wagon.

" That is so, Libby. Good thing tomorrow will be our day to be first in line and we shouldn't have to eat the dust. This afternoon we can climb inside the wagon and keep away from some of it.

"Nancy, it's so thick and the wagons are so noisy I can hardly hear you."

"Well, I don't think Mamma had any trouble hearing you last night when you told her about me dancing with Mason Connors."

"I'm sorry Nancy. I know I was a tattletale. Next time I am going to think twice before I run and tell."

"That would be a good idea Libby."

Libby bowed her head. She walked along with her head down and her bare feet scuffing up the thick dust. She felt a touch on her shoulder and heard Nancy say softly. "It's all right Libby. You were worried about me and I know you wanted to help me. Mason is a nice man and I think you will like him when you get to know him. Don't worry. I will always love you as my little sister no matter who I meet or get to know."

Libby stopped, raised her head and looked ahead at the long string of white topped wagons moving across the endless prairie. "What a long way to Oregon," she said.

"Yes," said Nancy. "And what a lot of dust there is before we get there."

Papa drove the mules over the dusty trail. They bowed their necks and dug in their hooves and made their way slowly, pulling the heavy wagon. Will walked beside the freight wagon cracking his long whip every now and then to urge the slow moving oxen along. The sun moved up across the sky pouring heat down onto the wagon train. Sweat stained the backs of Papa and Will's shirts and Libby and Nancy brushed their faces with their hand smearing dust into streaks of mud.

Nancy suddenly laughed as she looked at Libby's face.

"Libby, your face is as muddy as a tin pan in a mud hole. You have wiped the dust until you have muddy streaks up and down your face."

"Ha, ha, ha, Nancy. You have the same thing on your face."

The two girls both laughed so hard they bent bent over and held their sides.

Papa called out, "What's the trouble girls?"

Will answered, "They're just funnin Mr. Campbell. All's well. They just got dirty faces, that's all."

"Hoo-ah", called out Captain Jamison.

"Time for noonin I reckon," Will said.

"Papa pulled the mules off the trail and Will brought the Oxen and freight wagon along behind the family wagon. The oxen and mules were unhitched. The heavy ox yokes were unfastened and laid aside. Papa and Will led the animals to the river and let the thirsty animals drink.

Mama and Nancy set out cold beans cornbread, butter, and molasses for a cold lunch. There was no time to build a fire for nooning.

Jesse put a thick spoonful of butter on his cornbread then dipped it into a pool of molasses on his plate. He stuffed it in his mouth and said, "I am sure glad old Bitsy is giving us milk to make this butter. It is so-oo good."

"Yes, it is good, Jesse, but wait until your mouth is empty to tell us about it," said Mama. "And that reminds me, did you fill the churn Libby? It has been bouncing in the wagon all morning and should have some butter nearly made."

"I did it Mama, early this morning, just after Jesse milked Bitsy," said Libby.

"Hurrah for Libby," said Jesse. "She got something right."

Libby made a dash for Jesse but he was too quick and made a sharp turn around the freight wagon before Libby could catch him.

"I'll get you Jesse. You don't need to make fun of me. I do too get things right don't I Mama?"

"Of course you do, Libby and Jesse, don't tease your sister."

"Sorry Mama. Sorry Libby. But you are just so much fun to tease."

The nooning dishes were put away, Papa hitched the mules to the family wagon and Will put the heavy ,wooden yokes across the oxen's necks and fasted the bows.

"I would like to walk for awhile girls, if you two will ride inside the wagon with Ben," said Mama.

"Yes we will," answered Nancy. "We want to work on the doll for Liza. We can watch Ben too."

"Keep a close watch, especially if he rides on the seat with Papa. He could fall in front of the wagon wheels."

"We will Mama," said Libby.

"Let's get some scraps for clothes out of our quilt bags and you can use the embroidery thread I have to make a face for her," said Nancy.

The girls found a scrap of blue for a dress. Nancy drew a face for the doll and Libby worked with careful stitches to make eyes, nose and mouth.

The hot afternoon sun beat down on them but the bumpity bump of the wagon kept them awake.

"Ben!" Libby suddenly shouted, and dropped her sewing as she hurried to the front of the wagon. Ben was nodding his sleepy head and sat slumped against the corner of the wagon seat. The front wagon wheels rolled up over a big bush then suddenly came down again with a thud.

"Ee-eee," screamed Ben as he went flying out of the wagon.

Without a minute to think, Libby jumped behind him pushing him out of the way of the giant back wagon wheels and falling right behind him.

"Ben, Ben. Are you all right Ben?" Libby shouted as she patted her little brother's shoulder.

Ben lifted his head sending up a shower of dust as he shook his head to clear his nose and eyes. "I all right." He spluttered as he spit dust out of his mouth.

Papa stopped the mules and ran back to his children. "Are you hurt? Libby? Ben, are you hurt?"

He gently felt for broken bones and when he was sure there were none he lifted Ben in his arms and brushed his dusty hair and wiped his dirt stained face with his big red handkerchief.

Libby lay on the ground trying to lift herself. She pushed with her arms but felt something holding her tight. Her skirt was caught and she could not move. She screamed, “Help! ”

Papa reached down and pulled at her skirt but it was under one of the big wagon wheels.

“You are lucky my girl. That wheel just got your skirt and not your legs. We’ll get you free, ” Papa said.

Setting Ben on his feet he climbed up onto the wagon seat and drove the mules forward just far enough that the big wagon wheel rolled away from Libby’s skirt.

Nancy came quickly to Libby’s side. “Are you hurt Libby?”

“I think I’m fine.” She jumped up and down, took two hops then two more. “I am just the same as ever. No harm done once I dust off my skirt.” She brushed her hand across her skirt sending dust flying.

“Let’s get Ben into the wagon and wash his face and clean him up a bit,” said Nancy.

Mama and Papa came to make sure Ben and Libby were all

right. Papa put his big hand on Libby's shoulder and said, "Libby, you were a brave girl to jump out of the wagon and push your brother out of harm's way."

"Yes, a very brave girl, " said Mama.

"Were you afraid, Libby?" asked Nancy.

"I just thought about Ben. I didn't want him to get hurt. He's my brother."

Mama held her arm tight around Ben and sat next to Papa on the wagon seat. Libby and Nancy sat on their beds in the back of the wagon. Liza's rag doll was now finished except for sewing on some hair. Libby sat unwinding a short piece of rope then ran her fingers through the loose, curly strands.

"Do you have the hair ready Libby?" Nancy asked.

"Yes and it doesn't even look like rope now. It is more like strands of hair that has just been unbraided."

"Let me have it and I will sew it to the top of the doll's head."

She sewed on the hair and tied it back with a piece of dark, red yarn.

"Doesn't she look nice, Nancy?" Libby asked. "I wonder

what Liza will name her. It has to be an Oregon name. Maybe she can name her from a flower like Wild Rose or Violet."

"Whatever she names her will have to be her choice of names ," said Nancy. "I know it will be a special name that only Liza can give. her."

The family had camped, ate the evening meal, and dishes were washed and put away. Libby and Nancy walked to the Stamper wagon and called out to Liza.

Mrs. Stampers stepped down from the Stamper wagon and said, "Hello, girls. I will tell Liza you are here."

Liza dashed around the corner of the wagon and waved her arms in the air. "Welcome to the Stamper wagon," she said.

"Thank you Liza," said Nancy. We have something for you." She placed the rag doll into Liza's hands.

"Oh, she is so beautiful," Liza said as she held the doll out in front of her for her mother to see.

"She is really nice Liza ," said her mother."

"Oh, thank you so much," said Liza."

"Now, what are you going to name her Liza?" asked Libby.

Liza stood quietly for a moment thinking. She put two fingers across her lips then jumped up and down and said, "I know, I know. It's got to be an Oregon name and I know just the name for her. I will call her Stardust. Mama said Papa had stardust in his eyes when he decided to go to Oregon. Stardust might be a little long so I will probably shorten it to Star. That's a good name don't you think?"

"It's a good name, Liza," Nancy answered.

"I like it too," said Libby.

"I'm going to carry her in my apron pocket so she will be with me every minute," Liza said.

"Time for us to go to the wagon and get ready for bed," Nancy said.

"See you tomorrow, Liza," Libby called, "and Star too."

When the girls reached their wagon the campfire was burning low, the red embers glowing in the growing darkness. Far away a wolf's call echoed across the night then another and another with long, lonely wails.

"Let's get inside the wagon," said Nancy and they climbed up inside to their beds.

RATTLESNAKE

Libby and Liza walked beside the wagons as they moved slowly over the trail. Dust billowed up from the wagon wheels and the sun beat down on their sun bonnets. Libby brushed at the pesky flies that hovered around her face. Liza carried her rag doll, Star, in one hand and brushed away the flies with the other.

"Liza, do you think Star is going to like being out of your pocket all the time? She might get hot," Libby said.

"Oh, Libby, Star is just a doll. She is pretty but not really real. Not like you and me, flesh and blood real. She can't feel the sun. But just to make you happy I'll hide her in my apron pocket and the sun won't find her there."

"Good," said Libby. "Let's hurry. The wagons are pulling up for nooning."

"Whoa," called Papa to the mules, bringing them to a stop.

"Time for nooning," he called.

Nancy and Mama set out the food and tin dishes.

"We'll be stopping here for the rest of the day. It's time to rest the cattle and mules. They can graze here and we need to repair some wagon wheels", said Papa.

"Libby, as soon as you are finish eating, take the big basket and you and Ben fill it with buffalo chips. We will need them to cook supper," said Mama.

Libby got the big basket from the wagon. She took Ben's hand and walked across the grass looking for buffalo chips. This was a job Libby truly disliked. She didn't like to put her hands on the the dried pies of dung left by the buffalo and worst of all the pies sometimes turned out to be soft inside and the gooey, smelly buffalo dung oozed out from the inside breaking the hard crust on the outside and smearing her hands with buffalo dung.

"Come on Ben. Help me fill the basket. Can you find some chips?" Libby urged the little boy.

"I'll find some chips", Ben said and walked across the grass away from Libby

"Eee-eee!", he suddenly screamed.

Libby ran to the little boy, then stopped short as she stared at a large rattlesnake coiled and ready to strike. Its rattles buzzed a warning and the snake's head raised, its eyes like two dark beads and its tongue flicking in and out.

Libby was too scared to move. That snake could reach Ben

with its strike. Run, run fast, get away quick. Go for help she thought. No, no, I have to help Ben. If he runs that snake may strike.

"Stay still Ben. Stay right there and don't move." She slipped away to reach the big basket. She dumped out the buffalo chips, picked it up, slowly crept up to the snake, then stepped in front of Ben. With a quick toss she threw the basket over the rattler. She could hear the angry buzz of its rattles as it moved inside.

"Come on Ben. Let's find Papa." She took Ben's hand and ran as fast as the little boy's legs could go toward their camp.

"Snake, snake," she yelled as she approached the wagon. "There's a big rattlesnake under the basket," she called. Panting and out of breath she pulled Ben with her and collapsed against the wagon wheel.

Papa came running to the wagon and shouted "Where, where is the snake? Are you hurt Libby?" Papa asked.

Libby pointed in the direction of the big basket. "Over there Papa. He's under the basket. A big rattlesnake."

" We see rattlers all the time. No need to get excited. Just stay away from them," Papa said.

"But Papa it is so big and it was about to strike at Ben. I had to throw the basket over it".

"All right Libby. We will take a look at it.. Get the hoe out of the wagon and bring it along."

Libby climbed into the wagon and took out a long handled hoe that Mama had brought to use in her garden in Oregon. Papa reached for his rifle, which hung on the wagon bow and marched with Libby toward the big basket.

When they reached the basket they could hear the big snake rattle.

"Now Libby, give me the hoe and we will see what happens when we get the basket off this critter."

Libby handed the hoe to Papa and he raised it high above his head then threw it hard against the middle of the basket. The basket turned over on its side. The giant rattlesnake crawled toward them then coiled again sticking up its vicious head and shaking its rattles fiercely.

"You are a big fellow and dangerous too. You are too close to our camp for me to let you go," Papa said.

He raised his rifle and pulled the trigger, blasting the snake, sending its head in one direction and his tail in the other.

"That's the end of that rattlesnake and it won't come crawling up to Jesse's bedroll under the wagon tonight."

Libby walked beside Papa back toward the campsite and was quiet for a moment. When Papa didn't say anything more she asked softly, "Papa did I do the right thing, putting the basket over the snake?"

Papa put his big hand on Libby's shoulder. and said. "Libby, you did a brave thing and saved your brother from that angry snake. That big snake's strike could have reached Ben and its bite would have surely killed your brother."

Libby gave a little skip and reached for Papa's hand on her shoulder. Papa carried his rifle on his right shoulder and held on to Libby's hand with his other hand. All at once he stopped short.

"Guess our work isn't done yet Libby. We have to go back for the basket and fill it with chips for supper."

They turned around and went back for the big basket. Libby's shoulders shook as she looked at the dead snake lying in the dirt. She quickly picked up the basket and ran away from the snake a short distance and started filling the basket with chips.

Papa laid his rifle on the ground and helped fill it. When it was full he lifted his rifle on to his shoulder and took hold of one handle of the basket. Libby reached for the other. They carried it to camp where Mama was getting ready to make a supper fire. Papa sat down on the ground nearby to rest and told Mama about the big rattlesnake and about how brave Libby had been.

Mama hugged Libby and said, "Libby, you saved your brother."

She reached for Ben and hugged them both in her warm arms.

At bedtime Libby lay in her bed thinking about the snake and could not go to sleep. Far away the wolves called, sending their wail into the night. Libby pulled the covers tight under her chin and reached out and touched her sister Nancy whose even breathing told her that she was asleep. She felt safe beside her sister and she knew that Ben was safe and sound asleep in the big tent with Mama and Papa.

***

The sun beat down on the wagons as they made their way over the dusty trail. Libby and Liza walked together behind the Campbell wagons.

"I don't like this old hot sun, do you Libby?" Liza asked, as they dug their bare feet into the thick dust along the edge of the trail.

"No, not at all. Although it is better than those sticky old cactus we step on sometimes. Nancy had to pick some out of my feet last night."

"I wouldn't think Nancy had any time for that. She has been going to visit Mason Connors and his family a lot from what I see," said Liza.

"Oh, Liza. She is just being friendly. You know Nancy tries to be nice to people and Mason Connors' mother has been sick. Nancy has been going to help out."

"Is that why she walked by the river with Mason last night?" Liza asked and put her hand over her mouth and giggled.

"Well, I guess she can walk if she wants to. If Mason Connors comes along that is his business I guess," answered Libby.

"Oh, now, don't go gettin all huffy. I was just havin some fun. You know how it is. Romance gets everybody noticing things. Do you think Mason is Nancy's beau?"

"Maybe you can ask Nancy. How would I know? I don't go around spying on people," said Libby.

"Just be watchful. You don't have to spy but don't keep

your eyes closed either. You can learn a lot by just watching people Libby."

A rumble of thunder rolled across the prairie and the two girls turned to look at the dark clouds building up at the edge of the horizon behind the wagon train. The girls walked on, keeping up with the slow moving oxen as they plodded through the thick dust. The wagon wheels squeaked, bullwhips cracked and drivers shouted, "Giddy up! Get in there. Gee! "Haw!" as the wagons inched on under the darkening sky.

A sharp crack split the air and a bright, red dagger of lightning streaked across the sky. It frightened the two girls who screamed as they ran for their wagons. Giant raindrops pelted their dusty arms and legs. The wagons circled beside the trail. There were shouts and clanging of chains as the circle was completed.

"Get those oxen out of their yokes. Bring Maggie and Bitsy inside the circle," shouted Papa.

Libby's sun bonnet was wet by the time she reached the wagon and climbed inside. Nancy, Mama and Ben were already there. They stood by the pucker hole and looked out at Papa and Jesse using chains to fasten the wagons to stakes in the ground then chaining the wagons together. The wind was beginning to blow hard and the wagon covers flapped up and down as the rain poured over the top and down the sides . Mama pulled the strings tighter to make the pucker hole small so the rain didn't pour inside.

Papa and Jesse crawled inside the wagon, their shirts and pants soaking wet, their boots squishing water and their hair dripping as they clutched their hats to save them from the fierce wind.

"Worst storm I ever saw," said Papa. "I hope the chains hold the wagons and keep them from turning over."

" The wind is a howling monster," said Jesse and he sat down on the floor of the wagon.

"Are we safe Mama?" asked Libby in a small, frightened voice.

"Mama held Ben tight around the shoulders as if the wind might pick him up and carry him away. "We can pray Libby. Close your eyes and pray to God that he keeps us safe."

The wind blew against the wagon, rocking it from side to side. Rain poured over the canvas cover and and crept into the wagon onto the bedding and clothes. The barrels of meal and flower and their tight lids were stained dark from the water. Libby stood beside Mama and Ben. Her wet clothes and the cold air made her shiver.

Papa stood looking out the small pucker hole. "She's slowing down some. The chains are going to hold the wagons. No telling where the cattle will get to. I hope Bitsy is inside the corral. We need that milk cow just about as much as anything."

The rain and wind stopped but the water around the wagons stood in pools. Papa and Jesse waded through it, their boots squishing water as they took off the chains from the wagons and then went looking for the oxen and Bitsy.

Mama and Nancy started putting things right inside the wagon. The things that were soaking wet they wrung and spread out. They set up the tent and put the driest blankets down on the damp mattresses for the night's sleeping. They found the cooking pans and with the few sticks of dry kindling and buffalo chips they had saved, made a fire for supper.

Libby walked around the circle of wagons looking for Bitsy. They would all miss Bitsy's fresh milk and good butter if she wasn't milked. Libby looked behind and around all the wagons but there was no Bitsy. She stepped across the family wagon's tongue and shaded her eyes with her hand, looking out across the wide prairie. The sky was still cloudy and shadows edged around the rise just across from the circle of wagons. Could

Bitsy be over there, Libby wondered. If she walked a little further maybe she could see her. I'm not supposed to leave the camp without asking but I won't go very far and I will come right back thought Libby and she looked back at Mama and Nancy working at the camp fire. She ran toward the rise wrapping her arms together to keep warm. She wouldn't take time to get her cape and bonnet. She hurried toward the rise. She would need to get to the top to see if Bitsy was on the other side. Mama and Papa would be so proud if she found Bitsy.

She ran until her breath was coming fast and hard. Her feet skimmed over the hard dirt as she wove through the tall sagebrush. When she reached the top of the rise she looked in all directions but she could not see Bitsy. She walked down the opposite side just to make sure Bitsy wasn't hiding in the sage brush. She heard a swish, swish coming from a clump of sage brush. She hurried toward it. There was Bisty swishing her tail against the sagebrush.

Libby took off her apron and tied the strings around Bitsy's neck. She led her back up the rise. When she reached the top she looked in the direction she thought she had left the wagons. There was nothing there except empty prairie and the ever present clumps of sagebrush.

She hurried down the rise. Maybe when I get closer, she

reasoned, I can see the white wagon covers. She walked on pulling Bitsy behind her. After each step she peered across the empty prairie. There were no wagons anywhere.

She stopped and stood thinking. I have to see them soon. They were just across from the rise. But as she looked back the way she had just come she could see no rise at all. Where am I? Am I lost? Should I stop right here? Maybe I should stay put. Maybe I should wait for Papa and Jesse to come and find me. She tied Bitsy to a tall clump of sage brush and sat down on the ground to wait.

***

Shadows gathered in the low places and soon the light was almost gone. Libby stood and hugged Bitsy to keep warm. She could hear the rustle of small animals making their way through the sagebrush. She checked around her to make sure there were no rattlesnakes. As the darkness closed in around her, she could hear coyotes calling far away. Then a different call sounded nearby. She shivered and clutched Bitsy tighter. She knew that call. That was a wolf call and it was close. She turned to see two bright eyes shining in the dark behind the sagebrush. Libby quickly untied the cow and clung to the apron holding her.

"If that wolf comes to get us, Bitsy. I'll drop this apron and you run for your life. Do you hear me Bitsy?"

Bitsy answered with a long bawl and pranced around in circles as Libby held tight to her apron. She let out a loud whoop and flapped her skirt up and down. When the bright eyes didn't move she started swishing a piece of sagebrush back and forth. The eyes were still there and she heard an angry growl.

Then she remembered. She was the hand whistling champ of her old school. She closed here fists and blew on the tiny hole she had made. She blew as hard and as long as she could. A high piercing whistle screamed out into the night. Hearing it, Bitsy plunged back and forth against the sagebrush and let out a long protesting bawl. Libby looked for the eyes and they were gone.

"Thanks be to God. I hope that wolf is still running, Bitsy."

She stood by Bitsy, her arms around her neck as Bitsy stood patiently still. "I hope it's not much longer girl. Somebody will surely come."

She waited and waited and at last heard voices and hoof-beats growing louder. There he was, Jesse riding Maggie, and right behind him on Caleb, one of the big mules, was Papa.

"Daughter, thanks to that whistle of yours and Bitsy's bawling we have found you. You have worried your poor Mama more than any daughter should. Why oh why did you leave camp?"

Libby put her hands over her face and sobbed with great racking sobs. Jesse jumped down from Maggie's back, put his firm hands around her waist and said, "Up you go little sis. We are sure glad old Bitsy has a loud bawl and I am glad you learned that sharp hand whistle. Otherwise, we might still be out there chasing shadows on this dark prairie." With a swift boost he set Libby behind the saddle on Maggie's back then tied a rope around Bitsy's neck and secured it to his saddle horn.

They rode without talking with just the sound of hoof-beats as they rode across the prairie. Libby could feel the wind in hair as she clung to Jesse's waist. Fireflies danced around them and they could smell smoke from campfires. Soon they could see the bright sparks from the fires shooting up from the wagon encampment. The white wagon covers stood out in the dark and they soon found their own wagons.

Mama ran toward them with outstretched arms. "You found her. Oh, praise the Lord. We have been so worried Libby. We thought the Indians had you."

"Mama, I never even saw an Indian. I was trying to help

find Bitsy."

"Oh, Libby, never ever leave camp by yourself again. Do you hear?"

"I do Mama and I never ever will, I promise."

Papa and Jesse took Maggie and Caleb for water and feed and Mama filled a plate with buffalo stew for Libby. She ate every bit as if she had never tasted anything so good.

Mama leaned down and gave Libby a hug and a warm kiss on the check. "Tomorrow we are going to have to talk about this and decide your punishment. Goodnight now" She reached her warm arms around Libby and gave her another big hug.

Libby dressed in her nightgown and sat quietly on her bed in the dark.

Nancy reached out from her bed and said, "I'm glad you are safe Libby. We were so worried."

"I am glad too, Nancy. I was scared, really scared. I saw the eyes of a big old wolf. I scared him away with my whistle and Bitsy's bawling." She reached across to Nancy and hugged her big sister then snuggled down under her covers and was soon asleep.

***

The next morning Libby slowly climbed out of bed. Sunlight was streaking through the back of the wagon and she could hear the noises from the camp, the bellowing of animals and shouts from men. She dreaded talking to Mama and Papa about getting lost.

When the family had finished breakfast Mamma took Libby's hand and led her to the back of the wagon. Papa was there waiting.

"Libby, you disobeyed an important rule yesterday," said Mama.

"So that you remember Libby, we want you to stay at our camp until we reach Ft. Laramie. We hope that it will help you remember that you need permission to leave our camp. It won't be easy, Libby," said Mama. "When everyone else goes off to the dance or singing or storytelling, you will want to go but you must stay with our wagon.

There will be no visiting for you either. You can let Liza come to see you but you are not to leave our wagon to visit her."

"Think you can do that daughter?" Papa asked.

Libby's head was bowed and without looking up, nodded to let Papa know that she knew she must do as he said.

"Do you have anything to say daughter?" Papa asked.

"Papa, how far is it to Ft. Laramie?"

"A long way Libby and you will be getting pretty tired of this wagon before we get there. We will reach Chimney Rock and Scotts Bluff, then Ft. Laramie," said Papa.

"It must be a long way and take days and days, Papa?"

"Yes, it will take many days." answered Papa

"What will I do all that time at our wagon?" asked Libby.

"You can help with camp chores. Chores always makes time go faster. You can work on your quilt too, Libby. Of course Liza can come see you and you girls can play around the campsite," said Mama.

Captain Jamison called,"Wagons ho!"

The family started on the trail again. Libby walked beside the family wagon with her head bowed and her sunbonnet pulled forward to cover her face. The dust puffed up around her feet, she shivered from the early morning chill and pulled her shawl tight. As she plodded along she thought about what a long time it was going to be before they reached Ft. Laramie. To cheer herself up, she reached down and picked a tall blue flower, lifted it to her nose, and smelled the sweet, fresh bloom.

It made her think of Grandma's garden and she wondered how Grandma and Grandpa and Greyboy were getting along.

The wagons pulled into a circle after a long dusty day of traveling. The animals were unhitched and watered and left to graze. Supper fires were started and meals made ready.

"I am going to Mason's family camp this evening," Nancy said at supper. "They are having a dance and sing-a-long. They have invited us."

"All right, a real good thing," said Jesse.

"I might like to hear some good hymns," said Mama. I think I might go and sit for a spell. "

"Guess they might need a caller for the dance," said Will. "Redtop might come and call one of his twisters and give them boys a reason to swing the girls till the calico cracks. "

Libby gave a deep sigh. She would like to go to the dance too. She wished she could see Nancy and Mason Connors dancing. He must be sweet on Nancy. But no, she wasn't going to any dance. It was still a long way to Ft Laramie and she had to stay in their camp until they reached it.

A RIDE ON MAGGIE

Libby made things neat around the camp as the others hurried off to the Connors' campsite. Only Papa stayed behind to check the wagon wheels and brush down the mules and check them for harness rubs on their backs. Libby sat outside on one of the ox bows. She watched fireflies blink around the camp and heard a coyote howl in the distance. She listened as the fiddle music started up at the Connor's camp and floated through the night air. She shifted her feet and dug her bare toes into the soft dust. It would be fun to be dancing. Liza was probably there and Jesse would be dancing with every girl there who would dance with him.

She sat up and walked to the wagon and sat down on the wagon tongue for awhile. The chains squeaked as she stood up on the tongue to get a better look. Maybe she could see the light from the Connors' camp if she stood higher.

She couldn't see the Connors' camp but she stood very still for a moment. There was a swish, short and quick. She stared into the darkness beyond the wagon. She saw something move. It was dark but she could see a dark figure moving. Then she heard Maggie's whinny. She saw her plunging her front legs up in the air. On her back was a rider with long hair whipping in the wind as he rode away into the night.

"Indians!" she gasped. "Indians have got Maggie," she shouted.

Where was Papa? Maybe she should run to the Connors' camp and get Jesse. No, she had promised Mama and Papa that she would not leave camp. What could she do? She was the school's hand whistling champ and that was what she could do. She folded her hands together and blew as hard and as long as she could. Her whistle shrilled through the night air and even the camp dogs joined in barking in a chorus of yelps.

Jesse came running around the corner of the wagon. "I'd know that whistle anywhere and no mistake," he said . What's up Libby? What's wrong?"

"Oh, Jesse, an Indian came and rode away on Maggie. Maggie nickered and pawed the air but he rode her away into the dark," said Libby.

"I"ll borrow Mason Connor's horse and go after her," said Jesse, and he ran fast toward the Connors camp.

Soon the air was filled with shouts and whinnies of horses . Mothers put children in wagons and men lit lanterns and got out their guns. Jesse borrowed a horse, and left with Red Top the guide, Mason Connors, and Papa.

Mama and Nancy climbed into the wagon with Libby and Ben. They sat quietly listening and waiting. Finally they heard Caption Jamison shout.

"The camp is clear. No more Indians. It's safe to go to bed. It was more than likely a lone Indian horse thief."

***

Libby and Nancy buried their heads in their pillows and drifted into uneasy sleep. Mama sat in the rocker with Ben on her lap and waited through the dark night for Jesse and Papa and the others to return.

When Maggie's whinny came from outside the wagon, Libby sat up quickly. She hurried to the pucker hole. Riders were coming toward the circled wagons. They trotted down the dusty trail in the early morning light. Jesse leaned over Maggie's neck and urged her ahead of the others. Maggie's mane flew out in a dark cloud over Jesse's arm as he patted her neck urging her home. When they reached the wagon Maggie danced around in a circle as Jesse held her with his hand on her bridle.

"She is still excited," Jesse said. "She'll settle down after we wash and brush her down.

Tell you what, Libby, it was because of your whistle that I was able to get her back from that Indian. If you help me groom her and get her back in good shape I promise I will teach you to ride her."

"Oh, Jesse, you would let me ride Maggie?"

"Well, I figure you are big enough and lots of girls on the trail are riding horses. The way I figure it, one good turn deserves another. You sure did me a good turn tonight. If you hadn't whistled that Indian would have my horse for keeps. The way it was, Red Top followed his trail and we surrounded him and aimed our rifles straight at him. He jumped off Maggie and skedaddled about as fast as a wisp of wind. He is long gone back to where he came from we hope. Captain Jamison said he would post a double watch tonight just in case he gets brave and tries his luck again."

" Fill the water bucket and set it on Mama's breakfast fire to get warm," Jesse said. We don't want to surprise Maggie with a splash of cold water. She has had enough excitement for awhile."

Libby filled the water bucket and hurried to the the smoldering breakfast fire and set the tin bucket over the red coals. She ran back to watch as Jesse brushed down Maggie's rough coat until it was shiny and smooth.

"Take this brush and get the tangles out of her mane and tail. Talk to her softly and don't come up to quick and startle her," said Jesse.

Libby. spoke softly to the mare as she walked up slowly.

"Ho, Maggie, that's a good girl. I just want to help you and get your mane and tail cleaned up and get those burrs out for you."

She reached out her hand and softly touched the mare's shoulder. She could smell the mare's sweat and the dust from her tangled mane. She patted her neck gently.

"There Maggie, I can brush you now."

Maggie turned her head and sniffed at Libby's shoulder then turned her head back as if to say, you are all right. I know you.   Slowly Libby pulled the brush through Maggie's mane.

" I'll finish up brushing her tail and you get that bucket of water and we will give her a wipe down with that rag I have hanging on the wagon tongue. I don't think she is going to be worried about that Indian anymore once we wipe her down ," said Jesse.

Libby hurried to get the water bucket warming on the

breakfast coals.

"Get the rag on the wagon tongue and use it for a pot holder Libby," called Jesse.

Libby wrapped the rag around the bucket handle and carried the warm water to Jesse. "It isn't too hot, Jesse. I tested it. The bucket got hot but the water is just right."

Jesse dipped the old piece of shirt into the water and wrung it out then gently wiped down Maggie's coat. Maggie nuzzled Jesse's shoulder then whinnied softly. "See, she likes it . That warm water feels good doesn't it girl?"

When Jesse finished washing down Maggie, Libby cleaned up the bucket and put it away and hung up the rag to dry. She stood watching as Jesse led Maggie around the campground then back to the wagon.

" She seems no worse off from that Indian scare," said Jesse. "Guess it's time for me to keep my part of the bargain. Are you ready for a little riding lesson, Libby?"

"For real, Jessie?" asked Libby.

"This is as good a time as any. Maggie is all cleaned up. Come on over and let's see what you can do."

Libby inched forward, her bare toes making trails of dust as she dragged her feet along and she put her hands behind her back and walked with stiff knees to Jesse's side.

"Don't be afraid, Libby. Just go slowly with your moves until Maggie recognizes you. Now, we'll put you on Maggie's back without the saddle so she gets to know your smell and the feel of you. I'll make a step up for you with my hands. You can ride astride. No side saddle business for you even if you are a girl. Maggie isn't used to it. Up you go now."

Libby slipped her foot into the Jesse's hand and slung her leg over Maggie's back. Jesse held the mare's head with a firm grasp of her bridle .

"You're up Libby. Pretty good job for a girl I would say. Now hold on to her mane and I'll walk her around our camp so she gets used to you on her back."

Libby clung to Maggie's dark mane and leaned forward. Maggie was so tall and the ground was so far down. She closed her eyes because she felt a little dizzy.

"Relax, Libby," Jesse said . "Trust Maggie. Feel her soft back and her powerful muscles moving. She knows you are there and she is ready to giive you a nice ride.

Libby straightened her shoulders and extended her arms so she could grasp Maggie's mane. She could feel the air rush by her face as Maggie moved along. She pressed her legs against Maggie's sides and felt her strong muscles move smoothly forward then back. She smiled as she looked out at the camp of white wagons and the slow dying breakfast fires. She watched as Jesse took long strides ahead to lead his gentle mare around camp.

When he stopped Libby asked, "We're back so soon?"

"Yep, it's getting time to move out and we need to give old Maggie a rest. She's had a pretty big time of it. It seems she is pretty much settled down but I'll bet she won't forget that Indian and I'll bet he won't have any luck getting that close to her again. Slide down now Libby. You did a good job."

"Even if I am a girl?" Libby asked as she ducked her head down and smiled.

"That's right," said Jesse. "Boy or girl it's all the same to Maggie when someone treats her right. You have a good touch with horses Libby, and Maggie can tell. We'll have another lesson tomorrow night when we camp."

***

When the wagons moved out, Libby walked beside Liza next to the Campbell family wagon. Liza had her rag doll Star in her apron pocket.

“Look, Libby. Star is getting a bouncy ride just like she was riding in the wagon. I’m stomping over this old brush and bouncing her every step. I think I’ll hang on to her just in case she falls out of my pocket,” said Liza.

Libby tugged on the strings of her sunbonnet pulling them loose from under her chin. “It sure is hot all ready. I am glad you have the energy to stomp cause I feel like my feet are nearly glued to this old dirt I’m walking through. I’m glad you have a doll to keep you company, Liza. Do you suppose that Indian girl still has Tessie?”

“ If she does I hope she takes good care of her. I like Star but Tessie will always be my favorite doll . I have said good-by to her forever I expect,” Liza said frowning as she looked up into the bright sun.

“See that hill ahead? I think I see somebody up there,” she said and reached for Libby’s arm. “Could be an Indian up there, Libby,” she said squeezing Libby’s arm Both girls stopped and looked up to a high mound ahead on the right side of the trail.

“Look, I think that might be a horse up there with an Indian on its back,” Liza whispered.”

"Where?" asked Libby. "I don't see anything."

"I know I saw something up there and it looked like an Indian to me. I'm going to run tell Pa," Liza said and she ran ahead, leaving dust clouds behind her flying feet.

Libby walked slowly waiting for Mama to catch up to her. Mama came with her apron folded full of sticks she had collected for the night's supper fire.

" Where is Liza, Libby? Weren't you girls walking together today?" asked Mama.

"Liza said she saw an Indian way up there on that hill. I looked but I didn't see anything. She ran to their wagon to tell her Pa."

Mama shaded her eyes with her hand and looked up at the hill. " I don't see anything up there either. It is a good thing she went to tell her Pa. Red Top and Captain Jamison can keep a careful watch in case there may be Indians near."

Libby could hear the crack of Will's bullwhip as he sent it flying over the oxen's heads. They moved slowly, pulling the heavy freight wagon.

"The oxen seem to be slow today. I think they are looking poorly since we haven't found good grass," said Mama. I hope we can find grass and water tonight when we camp."

"Mama, today Jesse let me ride Maggie just around our camp. He said I could ride again tomorrow night when we camp. Do you suppose I could ride away from our camp for just a little way so I can learn to ride Maggie. It isn't far enough to ride just around our camping place. Maggie takes about three steps and we are back where we started. Please Mama, may I go with Jesse just around the circle of wagons?" Libby pleaded.

"So Jesse is letting you ride Maggie is he? That's a good thing. A girl needs to know how to ride in this wild country. But Libby, you have caused us so much worry. We want you to stay safe and remaining at our camp spot is the best thing to keep you safe. Papa and I have decided you need to do that." Mama answered.

"But Mama, how can I ride if I can't go anywhere. Jesse will watch for me. He knows how to keep me safe."

"So you and Jesse are friends now are you? I'm glad you and your brother are getting along. I will talk this over with Papa. Perhaps he will agree to your riding with Jesse."

INDIANS COME TO TRADE

It was early evening when the wagons circled in a grassy area near the Platte River. The oxen were relieved of their heavy yokes and the mules unharnessed and turned out to graze. Libby stayed near the Campbell wagons. She could hear Liza calling across the big circle of wagons but she didn't answer. She would not leave her family's camp spot as she had promised. She hoped Mama would ask Papa about riding Maggie away from their camp. She walked to the supper fire to help Mama and Nancy.

They were sitting down on the grass to eat when all at once, a tall Indian dressed in fringed leggings and moccasins was suddenly standing behind Jesse.

Jesse jumped up and stood facing the Indian and with a loud voice shouted,

"What do you want?"

The Indian motioned for biscuits and meat. Mama came quickly and held the pan of biscuits toward the Indian.

"Ump," the Indian grunted and reached out with his big hands and filled them with biscuits. He stuffed them in his mouth one after the other until they were all gone. He reached for the meat in the hot frying pan, then jerked back his hand and took a long spear, stuck it into a piece of meat, letting it dangle in the air to cool, and finally put it to his mouth.

Libby crept to her mother's side and Jesse and Nancy came closer, standing on either side of Mama.

Papa said, "Might as well eat what's left folks. Looks like we are going to have some more company soon."

Libby looked around the camp and saw many Indians around the circle of wagons eating and trading with the people.

Libby had just finished eating when an Indian woman dressed in a long, fringed buckskin dress came to their camp. A young girl with long dark braids and a beaded buckskin dress and moccasins followed behind her. The woman held up a pair of moccasins and pointed to the wagon.

"She wants to trade the moccasins," said Nancy. I think they will fit me. I will go see if I can find something to trade. She looked inside the wagon and came out with a string of blue glass beads and a long red hair ribbon. She held them out toward the Indian woman who placed the moccasins in Nancy's hands and took the beads and ribbon smiling as she bowed her head.

The tall Indian man took the little girl's arm and walked with her to face Mama. He pointed to the biscuit pan and then to the little girl.

"I have no more biscuits," Mama told him.

"The tall Indian shook his head and gestured rapidly pointing from the pan to the little girl's mouth. The Indians then sat down on the grass to wait.

Mama hurried to build up the fire again and stir up the biscuit batter. She soon had biscuits baking in the dutch oven over bright red coals.

Libby and Nancy stayed close to Mama. Libby shoulders shook and she clenched her hands together in front of her. She whispered to Nancy. " Will they hurt us?"

"I don't think so," answered Nancy. "From their dress I think they are Sioux Indians and they are supposed to be friendly. We will stay close to help Mama. Papa and Jesse are in the wagon getting their guns in case of trouble. Stay still and stay quiet."

Libby stood near the smoldering cooking fire. She could feel the heat from the fire and turned her face away. She saw the Indian family sitting on the grass waiting for more biscuits. The girl had something in her hand. Libby walked closer to better see what it was. She could see a doll dressed in a brown leather dress with dark hair and a wooden face. She pressed her hand over her mouth but it didn't silence the loud, "No!"

She ran toward the Indian girl yelling, "That's my friend Liza's doll. That's Tessie. I know that doll," she said, pointing to it and waving.

The Indian girl slid closer to her mother and clutched the doll against her chest. Libby reached down to grab the doll. Strong hands closed around her shoulders. Libby pulled back but was caught fast by the tall Indian man. She kicked and twisted from side to side and screamed.

"Papa!" She ducked her head and stomped on the Indian's moccasins and screamed again. "Help!"

She looked up to see Papa standing in front of her pointing his rifle at the tall Indian. Right behind him was Jesse with his rifle pointed at him too.

"Daughter, step away, " Papa said.

The Indian did not take his hands away and Libby was held tight.

Jesse fired his rifle in the air. The Indian pushed Libby forward, she stumbled and went flying to the ground. The

Indian family backed away then disappeared into the shadows. Men came running with their rifles. Women and children ran to the wagons to find cover inside. Other indians ran for their ponies and were soon gone in a cloud of dust. Libby sat on the ground sobbing until Papa picked her up and put her in the wagon. Nancy came and put her arms around her until her sobbing had stopped. Mama washed her face with a damp cloth and Nancy brushed off her dusty skirt and apron. She helped her lie down on her bed, and removed her worn dusty shoes. She patted Libby's shoulder and said, "You are safe now Libby. The Indians are gone."

There was shouting and loud talking outside the wagon as the men from the wagon train looked for Indians that might be hiding outside the circle of wagons.

When the voices were no longer loud and excited, Mama looked out of the back of the wagon to see Papa and Jesse standing nearby talking quietly to Liza's father, Mr. Stampers.

Mama stepped outside to tend to the supper dishes. Nancy got a cup of water for Libby and put it in her hands.

"Don't worry Libby," she said. "The Indians are gone and I don't think they will hurt us. They just wanted to get food and trade."

Libby sipped the water and then lay quietly thinking about the Indian girl who had Liza's doll. Liza would probably never see Tessie again.

There were voices outside the wagon and suddenly Libby heard someone shout, "That's the wagon of that girl who almost got us all killed. Her Pa should give her a good lickin."

Libby jumped up from her bed and peeped out the pucker hole. There was a tall, skinny boy with uncombed, dark hair talking to two other boys. Where had she seen that boy before with his worn clothes and dirty, bare feet? His mouth was turned down and he had a frown on his face. She had seen that boy before but where? Then she remembered. He had been in Independence on the day she and Liza had gone to see the peddler. He had called them a worthless bag of bones. How had he got into this wagon train?

Libby felt ashamed. Did everyone think of her that way? That she had caused trouble with the Indians? She slipped out of the wagon and walked quietly to find Mama. She helped her wash up the supper dishes and put things away. "They walked back to the wagon and Libby asked, "Mama do you think I started trouble with the Indians?"

"Do you think you did, Libby?" asked Mama.

"I just wanted to get Liza's doll back for her."

"What you did Libby was act before you took time to think. We are very lucky that the Indians left without causing us trouble and even now Captain Jamison is posting extra guards in case the Indians come back. You have to think of all the people in the wagon train before you do something to endanger us all. You will need to apologize for what you did. Captain Jamison will hold a meeting tomorrow morning and you will go and offer your apology. Goodnight now. You will be safe with the guards posted outside."

Libby turned her face to her pillow and sobbed. How could she face everyone in the wagon train at the meeting in the morning?

I APOLOGIZE

Libby was so sorry she had run to the Indian girl. She had just wanted to get Liza's doll. But what if the Indians had used their bows and arrows and the long spear the tall Indian man had carried? She lay thinking about what she would say for a long time. She would probably not get to ride Maggie either. Mama wouldn't ask Papa and if she did, Papa would never agree to her riding Maggie away from their camp. She heard Nancy come to the wagon and get into bed but she lay very still so that Nancy would think she was asleep and there would be no questions to answer.

The next morning Mama called from outside, "Time to go Libby."

Libby slowly pushed up from her bed and smoothed her clean apron and looked down at her worn shoes. She had wiped them clean from dust and put on her best pair of stockings. Nancy had braided her dark hair and tied blue ribbons at the ends of her braids. She wore her best blue gingham dress and white apron. She had washed with some of Nancy's rose petal soap and she could smell the fresh scent on her hands as she smoothed back the small, determined curls that escaped her braids. Slowly she climbed down from the wagon and looked up at Mama who stood waiting for her at the back of the wagon.

"Are you ready with your apology, Libby?" Mama asked.

"I am afraid Mama," Libby answered.

"It is not easy to admit making a mistake, Libby, but just say what is in your heart and tell the people that you are truly sorry. I think people will accept your apology."

The people from the wagon train had gathered inside the circle of wagons near Captain Jamison's wagon. The sun was up and warmed the cool morning air. Breakfast camp fires were now just red embers with lingering puffs of smoke sending out the smell of burning wood.

Captain Jamison called the meeting to order. The men and women stood quietly in their trail worn clothes, their sun burned faces looking up toward Captain Jamison. Children sat on a grassy knoll. Some boys were rolling and wrestling in the grass trying to avoid the cow pies left by the cattle.

Captain Jamison removed his broad brimmed hat and said, "Let us open our meeting with prayer. Will you lead us Doctor Whitman?"

Doctor Marcus Whitman stepped forward and removed his

hat. As if it were a signal the men in the group lifted their dusty and weather worn hats to uncover long hair that had not seen a barber shop in many weeks.

Libby stared at the man who was introduced as Doctor Whitman. Could it be the famous doctor who had started the settlement of Waiilatpu?

She heard the crowd quietly murmur, "Dr. Whitman. Dr. Whitman. It's Dr. Whitman."

Libby was so excited she didn't hear what Dr. Whitman said. She was thinking of the man who had come as a missionary to teach the Indians and had been one of the first pioneers to establish a settlement in the Oregon country. She tried to listen to the famous man's words but heard only, "Amen." He had finished his prayer.

Captain Jamison read names for the double watch that would be kept for the next night and told the people it would be required for another few nights since the incident with the Indians the night before. Liza felt so ashamed of herself she bent her head so that she wouldn't see anyone looking at her. She hoped there would be a lot of business for the people to discuss because she didn't want the time to come when she would have to speak. But there wasn't a lot of business and before she had time to think over what she planned to say Captain Jamison was calling her name.

"Now the little girl who was a bit too close to the Indians last night has something to say, Elizabeth Campbell."

Libby's feet stayed frozen to the ground until she felt Mama's firm hands on her shoulders that gently urged her forward. She looked down at her feet not daring to look up at the faces she passed on her way to the front of the group. Captain Jamison helped her climb up on a wooden crate. She looked out over the group of people who stood watching, shading their eyes from the bright morning sun.

The women standing slightly behind the men stirred and someone pushed toward the front. It was Liza. She carried a bouquet of wildflowers. She reached up and placed them in Libby's hands. There was a rumble of chuckles from the men and a few of the women clapped their hands.

Libby looked up and smiled. Maybe everyone didn't despise her. Maybe some even liked her. She was sorry for what had happened and she wanted to tell them so.

"My name is Elizabeth Campbell. I came here this morning to tell one and all that I am sorry for what happened last night. I am sorry if I caused anyone to be afraid. I wanted to get Liza's doll back for her and I thought it was wrong for the Indian girl to keep it. But I made a mistake. I was just thinking about myself and Liza. I didn't ask myself what the Indians might think and how I might get us all into trouble. I am truly sorry."

Libby bowed her head and clutched Liza's flowers as she walked away. Liza came running behind her and took hold of her arm. Just as they reached the edge of the group a foot came out across their path to trip Libby. Liza quickly pulled Libby aside and looking up they saw the dark haired, mean boy who called out.

"Yea, taint likely you crazy little bag-o-bones will have any sense."

The girls ran quickly to the Campbell's wagon. They climbed into the wagon and sat down on Libby's bed breathing fast from their run.

" Did you see that boy Libby?" Liza asked when she got enough air to speak.

"I know who that boy is," answered Libby. "That is the boy we saw in Independence when we went to see the peddler. He's the one that called us a worthless bag- o-bones. Now he called me a crazy little bag-o- bones."

"And he would have tripped you if I hadn't pulled you away

from that foot he stuck out in front of you. He is some piece of trouble I figure Libby. Let's stay clear of him from now on."

"I will Liza if I can at all but what if he intends to make trouble for me?"

"Well," Liza said and jumped up from the bed pumping her fist in the air. "This right here means trouble and he better watch out."

The girls fell across the bed in a fit of giggles, laughing so hard about Liza's small, thin arm threatening to do harm to the big, rough boy who had called them names.

***

"Hoah!"

The call came from Redtop in front of the wagon train. The wagons had started moving ahead. It was time for the long day to begin. Libby and Liza jumped from the back of the wagon just as Papa climbed up to the wagon seat.

"Bye, Libby. Got to go and catch up to our wagon," called Liza as she ran ahead.

Libby put one determined foot down after the other and walked beside the family wagon. The sun was bright and the air was hot. She could feel sweat rolling down her cheeks and her hair felt damp under her sunbonnet. She pushed her sunbonnet back and let it fall down her back, tying the strings together at the ends.

"Whee!" she said and puffed out her breath when she heard the call for nooning.

The wagons were pulled to a stop and Mama and Nancy set out the cold beans and bread. Libby filled the water pitcher with water from the barrel on the side of the wagon then filled the tin cups set out on the old quilt on the ground. Papa took off his wide brimmed hat and brushed his brow with his shirt sleeve.

"It's gonna be a scorcher this afternoon. It's plenty hot right now," he said as he sat down on a clump of grass. "It would sure be nice to have a cold cup of spring water. Redtop says we will reach a good spring by tonight and we will have all the cold water we need."

"Where is that fresh, spring water?" Jesse asked when he came riding up on Maggie.

He jumped off the mare and dropped the reins down to the ground. Maggie stayed still as she had been trained to do.

"I'll get you a drink Maggie," Libby said as she gently rubbled the mare's neck. "I know you are thirsty too."

"Thanks Libby," Jesse said and sat down on the ground. He

quickly drank a cup of water, then filled it again.

Maggie nickered as Libby set a bucket of water in front of her. The mare sniffed the water then drank from the bucket.

"Maggie doesn't mind if the water is warm. She is drinking every bit," Libby said .

"That's enough Libby," Jesse called. "Don't give her too much. She won't want to chase those stubborn critters all afternoon if she drinks any more. We have got plenty of work keeping the strays rounded up in the back. Maggie knows our cattle and she keeps em heading behind the wagons. I am lucky to have Maggie. She works with me real good," Jesse said and lay back with his arms under his head and his hat over his face.

They ate lunch in silence, in the shade of the big wagon, its canvas top shadowing the ground. The sun was nearly overhead and the hot rays reached all around the camp site. Pesky flies came to bite and kept Maggie stomping her hooves to scare them away.

Libby helped Mama and Nancy clean up the dishes and pack them. Little Ben settled down in the back of the wagon for a nap and Jesse rode away to herd the cattle at the end of the train. Papa climbed to the wagon seat and they were soon back on the trail. Mama, Nancy and Libby walked along beside the wagon. The high spirited mules bent their heads, their ears flicking against the dust and flies.

The oxen pulling the freight wagon walked slowly through the thick sand. Will cracked his long bullwhip over their heads and they patiently took one slow step after the other. The distance between the two wagons kept getting longer and longer.

Papa pulled the mules to a stop and waited for the freight wagon to catch up. Will came forward and looked up from his worn, wide brimmed hat and said, "Two of them oxen have got sore feet. They can hardly go. We better put some booties on em tonight. I'll pull out and wait till the end of the train cause they just can't go no faster."

"All right, Will," Papa said. "We'll fix em up tonight."

The train moved on slowly and eyelids drooped. Libby was so sleepy she could hardly take another step. but kept walking beside Mama and Nancy. They walked because it was too hard for the teams to pull extra weight in the heat and sand. Only Ben, who had awakened from his nap, rode beside Papa on the wagon seat.

When Libby thought she could not lift her foot to take another step, she heard Captain Jamison call to halt the train.

"Hoah"

Papa pulled the mules off the trail and followed the wagon in front to make a circle. The family all dropped to the ground exhausted. When Jesse brought a bucket of cold spring water to drink they filled their cups then filled them again

"Libby, you take Ben and fill up a basket with buffalo chips. Get it done quickly. We need to make supper."

Libby let out a little groan as she pushed up off her knees. She reached for Little Ben's hand and got the big basket from the wagon. "Come on Ben," she said. "We've got to get this job done."

They walked together until they could see the chips scattered over the ground. Libby bent over and reached with both hands then sent them flying into the basket.

"Here's one Libby," Little Ben called.

"Without looking up Libby answered, "Put it in the basket, Ben."

The basket was soon full but Libby wanted to make sure Mama had plenty so she piled them high above the top of the basket.

She had put her hand down on one last chip and heard a swish. She turned to see the basket tumbling over spilling half its chips then felt a damp, gooey, smelly mess cover her face and something pushing her to the ground. She stuck out her hands behind her to catch herself as she sat down on her bottom. She sputtered and blew to clear her mouth and nose and looked up to see the mean boy from Independence looking down at her and laughing.

"Serves you right, you worthless, little bag-o-bones," he said and laughed with a loud cackle.

There were other children gathering chips who came running to see what had happened.

When some of the boys started holding their sides and bending over laughing, Libby jumped up, her temper making her face red under the gooey mess. She ran to the boy and with all her strength, pushed against his back sending him sprawling face down in a soft buffalo chip.

"Now look who's laughing you mean, awful boy," Libby shouted. "And how does that buffalo chip you ate taste anyway?" she asked.

The children gathered around and laughed even louder and one of the boys pointed his finger and said, "She got ya, Charlie."

" I'll get you, you little beggar. If you weren't a girl I would smash you right here. Just wait. You wait. I'll get you and you'll be sorry of the day you ever laid eyes on this right here," and he pointed his finger at his chest poking it back and forth. He then turned and ran back toward the wagons.

Libby quickly refilled the big basket, took Little Ben's hand and dragging the basket, walked back to camp. She hurried to get water and soap to wash her face and hands before anyone had a chance to see her covered with messy buffalo dung. She scrubbed hard and rinsed off her soapy face with cold water. She smelled a lot better and the heat soon dried the spots she had washed off her dress.

Mama built a fire and soon had the coals hot enough to heat the dutch oven filled with bread. Nancy set out the butter she took from the churn in the wagon, made as the wagon bumped along all day. Libby put out the plates, tin cups, knives and forks.

BOOTS FOR OXEN

When supper was over Libby found Papa and Jesse cutting a piece of leather for the oxen's booties. They cut the buffalo hide booties for Baldy and Clementine then cut some long leather strips to use as ties.. Will tied white headed Baldy to the back of the wagon. He lifted each of his hoofs and cleaned out the dirt and small stones. He patted Baldy's neck and spoke gently.

"There Baldy. You're a good old boy."

Papa lifted Baldy's hoof and placed the piece of buffalo hide with the hair on the inside around the ox's hoof. While Papa held it in place Jesse wrapped a leather thong around the piece and tied it. They worked until Baldy had shoes covering his four sore feet.

Will brought Clementine and fastened her to the back of the family wagon with a chain. She was not happy and pulled back on the chain until the heavy wagon shook, rattling the tin dishes in the grub box.

"Woah, now Clementine," soothed Will. "Easy now. We want to fix you up," he said and rubbed the ox's neck.

Clementine let out a bellow and her dark red coat rippled over her giant shoulders. Will kept up a gentle caress over

Clementine's neck until she shook her head, settled quietly, and chewed her cud.

Papa and Jesse quickly put on the booties and tied them. Libby ran to bring the two oxen a pail of water. She washed away the dust from each ox's eyes and nostrils. Clementine thanked her by letting out a long bellow and Baldy added his thanks by blowing from his nostrils sending a spray of water out to dampen Libby's apron.

"That's all right Baldy. The drops of water will just make a nice mud on my dusty apron." She laughed as the big ox bobbed his big head up and down.

Libby put out the tin wash basin and a clean towel for the men to clean up their dusty arms and hands.

"Thank'e Little Miss. Mighty kind of you to help us get cleaned up," Will said.

"You're welcome," Libby said and felt all warm inside when she realized that Will had noticed she was trying to help.

There was dancing by their campfire in the evening. Libby sat with Liza and they clapped their hands to the music of the fiddle and banjo. Libby watched as Nancy whirled around with Mason Connors when Will called out, "Swing yer Partner."

"Nancy's still sweet on Mason Connors ," Liza said and giggled as she patted Libby's shoulder.

"Oh, I don't know. Could be she just wants to dance," answered Libby.

"It sure peers to me she likes him. She is looking up at him and smiling big as can be. You might get a new brother one of these days, Libby, " Liza said.

"I don't need another brother. I've got Jesse and Ben," said Libby.

"All the same, looks like things are going in that direction. I think they are sweet on each other," Liza said and jumped up and ran with her rag doll, Star, back to her family wagon.

Libby took one last look at her big sister Nancy who stood talking to Mason Connors at the edge of the firelight. She walked slowly to the Campbell's wagon. She dragged her bare feet through the dust as she thought about Nancy going away, maybe to a home of her own. She wanted Nancy to be happy but she hoped it would be a long time before she had to say goodby to her big sister.

Libby got ready for bed and lay listening to the far away wail of wolves. It was good to be safe inside the wagon. She wondered if she would see the mean boy again. He said he would get her. She wasn't afraid. She would be watching next time for someone behind her. There would be no more soft buffalo chips on her face.

***

Will and Jesse were yoking the oxen when Libby awoke to the sound of Jesse's voice.

"They are holding Will. The boots we put on last night should give Old Baldy and Clementine a rest from their sore hooves today."

"Yup, they ought to feel better today and their sore feet should have a chance to heal. They are good oxen and we aim to try and keep em healthy," said Will

As Libby climbed down from the wagon she watched Jesse ride away on Maggie to round up their stock. She was late to get breakfast. Everyone else had finished except Ben and he stood by Mama rubbing his eyes.

"Get yourself and Ben some mush and milk for breakfast, Libby. We will be starting soon." Mama said.

Libby poured fresh milk over two bowls of cornmeal mush and sat down with Little Ben to eat. When she was finished she took Ben back to the wagon and washed his face and combed his hair. She boosted him into the wagon and he climbed up on the wagon seat to sit beside Papa. When the wagons moved out, Libby fell into step beside Nancy as the wagons rolled over the trail.

"Do you like Mason Connors, Nancy?" asked Libby.

"Yes. Yes I do like Mason. He is a good dancer too. He is quite nice looking and I really hope he will be my beau," answered Nancy.

" I guess that answers my question about how much you like him. Seems to me you like him a lot."

"I do like him and I respect him too. He is nice to his mother and his two little sisters and he is a gentleman when he is with me. I hope it isn't the end of our friendship when we reach Oregon. Oh I wish, Libby, that things could be as we wish them to be. But who knows what is ahead for us? It is still a long way to Oregon."

Both girls walked along in silence. Libby thought about Nancy and Mason. She must be in love. They probably would get married but when? Libby hoped it would be a long, long time before Nancy went away.

It was a dry camp when the wagons stopped for nooning. Will and Jesse carried water from the water barrel for the oxen and mules to have a drink and Jesse also gave Maggie a drink. Libby filled the tin cups with water for the family, from the water barrel and they drank it quickly, thirsty for more but knowing they had to conserve water, did not ask.

When they had finished lunch they were soon back on the trail again. Will cracked his long whip over the oxen's heads and the big animals plodded on through the heat and dust. The mules flicked their ears, bowed their necks and pulled the big blue wagon. Papa and Ben bounced up and down on the wagon seat. Libby, Nancy and Mama walked beside the wagon, their bonnets tied to keep out the dust.

TROUBLE

"Libby, when we stop, I think you will need to gather more buffalo chips," said Mama.

"Ugg," answered Libby. "I don't like those oozy ones at all. That mean boy may try something. He said he would get me."

"Well, I wouldn't worry so much about him. I will tell Jesse to keep his eyes open for any trouble. You just get your job done. We have to have a fire for cooking. We don't want a cold supper tonight," Mama said.

Libby wiped her sweaty hand across her cheek and gave a long, sad sigh. "I will gather them for you Mama," she said.

"Don't worry, Libby," Nancy said, and she laid her hand on Libby's shoulder. "Mean boys like to brag and chances are his bragging is all that he will do. I will go with you if you like."

"No, you need to help Mama and I can do this myself," Libby answered.

"That's the spirit Libby. Of course you can. I will help Mama fix a good supper as soon as you bring us the chips."

Libby bowed her head and wiped a secret tear away. She didn't want her big sister to know how she hated this job.

Maybe the mean boy wouldn't show up. Another boy had called him Charlie. Well old Charlie had better watch out. She would be watching this time and there would be more soft buffalo chips just ready for a mean boy's face.

The wagons pulled into a circle for the evening. There was cold spring water nearby and grass for the animals. Mama held out the big basket.

"Here Libby. It's time to gather some chips for the supper fire."

Libby slowly extended her hand, took the basket, and did not look up at Mama.

"Go on now Libby," said Mama. "That mean boy is probably busy somewhere else."

Libby picked up the basket and walked just outside the circle of wagons where buffalo chips were scattered across the ground. She looked around her on both sides and then turned and looked behind her. There were three other children filling their baskets with chips but there was no mean boy anywhere in sight. She bent to pick up chips and pitched them into the basket. She moved ahead a little farther. The wind blew across the prairie and rustled the dry grass. Libby hurried back and forth to fill the basket.

"You ugly little ole gal. I've got somethin fer you," came a voice from right behind her.

Libby turned and screamed running as fast as she could toward a small ravine. Right behind her came Charlie dangling a long rattle snake from a green stick that was bent double and twisted around the snake's head.

"Don't do you no good to run sister. You can't out run old Charlie. You're gonna get what's comin to ya," he said as he closed the distance between them.

Charlie reached his arm back to throw the snake onto Libby but before he could release it, an iron grip enclosed his upper arm and Jesse shouted, "Hold on there. Drop that rattler right now."

The stick fell to the ground, the rattlesnake, loose once more, quickly glided toward some big rocks in the ravine. Charlie twisted free of Jesse's grip and ran to Maggie who stood where Jesse had left her. Charlie leaped onto the saddle and kicked his heels against Maggie's sides, urging her away toward the ravine.

"Come back here with my horse," Jesse shouted.

Hearing Jesse's voice, Maggie leaped up, pawing the air, trying to throw off the strange rider. Charlie gave her another mean kick and she went racing across the ravine, stumbling into a big hole, and falling with a loud scream.

Libby stood watching as Maggie lay on her side, struggling and flailing her free legs and raising her head again and again.

She saw Charlie scramble up from the dirt where he had been thrown. He ran to the horse and looked down at the deep hole where the mare's front leg was bent and broken. He wiped his wet cheeks with a dirty fist and snuffled his runny nose crying, "You blasted horse. Why did you run into this ditch? You dumb critter. You got me into big trouble now." He stood sobbing looking down at the struggling mare.

Jesse came running out of breath to the top of the ravine. Ignoring Charlie standing beside Maggie he charged down to his horse to look after her. She nickered softly as she raised her head when smelling her master's scent.

Jesse stroked her neck and crooned softly to her.

"There girl. Easy girl. Lay still girl. Good girl. My good little girl."

He stroked her until she let her head rest quietly on the ground and her legs lay still.

While he soothed his wounded horse Jesse looked around at

the terrible situation that had brought Maggie down. He turned to look for Charlie who had run to the top of the ravine.

Libby stood watching her big brother. He kept gently stroking his mare's neck. Maggie nickered in soft little sounds. Jesse looked up and Libby saw that he didn't have any tears but there was an angry and determined look in his eyes.

She ran to her brother's side and leaned against him as she looked down at the fallen mare. "Maggie's hurt Jesse. Let's help her up. Come on Jesse. We have to help her right now," Libby said as she pulled at Jesse's sleeve.

"Hush Libby. Maggie's leg is broken. Go get Papa and tell him to bring my gun."

"Why, Jesse? Why do you need your gun? That snake is gone."

Jesse stood up and faced his sister. He placed his hands on her shoulders and spoke softly.

"Libby, Maggie can never walk again. You know what that means. She can't live. The way we can help Maggie is to end her pain. Go now and get Papa."

Libby turned and ran up the bank of the ravine running right past Charlie. She ran across the prairie as fast as she could. The wind whistled in her ears and the loose hair from her braids blew across her face and into her damp eyes. She struggled over clumps of sage and grass but never stopped. She had to get help for Maggie.

When she reached the wagons she called, "Papa, Papa, we need help."

Mama and Nancy ran to her. Mama asked, "What's wrong, Libby? Are you hurt?"

"No, Mama. It's Maggie. She is hurt so bad. Jesse wants his gun."

"I'll get Papa," Nancy said and ran toward the big mules that Papa was watering.

Papa turned the mules lose to graze and came quickly to the wagon. He reached for his rifle and then Jesse's, hanging inside the wagon on hooks.

"Come Libby. Come show me where Maggie and Jesse are ."

Libby reached out her arm and pointed in the direction of the ravine she had just left. She had to trot to keep up with Papa's fast walk.

When they reached the ravine Papa hurried to Jesse's side. He was on his knees stroking Maggie, who was barely moving now.

Papa looked down at the mare and her twisted front leg. His eyes were sad. He looked down at Jesse trying to comfort his injured mare.

He placed his hands on Jesse's shoulder and said, "Son, I am sorry. Do you want me to do it? I will if you can't."

"No, Papa," Jesse answered. "I have to do it. Maggie has been so true, so good. I have to end her pain."

"All right then, " Papa said.

Jesse stood and it was then that Libby saw tears rolling down his cheeks. He brushed them away and reached for his rifle.

"Want us to stay with you?" Papa asked.

"No, Papa. I need to be alone with Maggie," Jesse answered.

"Let's go then, Libby. Let's head back to the wagons," Papa said.

They started up the bank of the ravine but stopped when they saw Charlie.

"You are Alvin Martin's boy aren't you?" Papa asked.

"Yeah, that's right. I didn't do nothin to that crazy horse.

She just went loco and jumped in that gully," he said.

"Well, we need to leave Jesse alone now. You need to come on back with us to the wagons," Papa said in a firm voice.

Charlie walked behind them all the way back to the wagons.

Papa said, "You go on to your wagon boy and we will get the answers to all of this later."

Charlie went slinking off away from the Campbell wagons and Mama and Nancy came from the cooking fire to ask about Jesse.

Nancy had found the big basket and brought back buffalo chips to make the supper fire. Supper was still warm and waiting.

"No need to wait for Jesse," Papa said. "He will be along after awhile."

They ate warm buffalo stew and corn bread and then sat by the fire. They didn't speak of the terrible thing that had happened to Jesse's beloved Maggie but Libby saw the sad faces of Mama, Papa and Nancy. She could tell from the way her lips tightened and her forehead wrinkled that her face looked sad too.

Even Little Ben climbed into Mama's lap and asked,

"Where's Jesse?"

They sat silently waiting and then it came, one long boom from the direction of the ravine. Papa stood up, put his hands in his pockets and walked away a distance. He turned his back and looked toward the ravine. Mama wiped her eyes with the corner of her apron and Nancy hid her face in her hands. Libby didn't bother to hide her tears. She just sat and let them run down her checks and on down to dampen the front of her dress. There would be no riding Maggie ever. What difference did it make if they reached Fort Laramie? It probably wouldn't matter now how good she was or how pleased Mama and Papa were with her. There would be no horse to ride. Maggie was gone.

It was dusk when they saw a lone figure walking slowly toward the wagons. His head was down and across his shoulder he carried his saddle and bridle, holding them with his right hand. In his left hand he carried his rifle. It was Jesse.

Libby stared to run toward him but before she could leave the campsite she felt Papa's hand on her shoulder.

"Not now Libby," he said. "Let Jesse have some time by himself."

Jesse walked by them without looking up and silently went to the freight wagon. Will was there and helped Jesse put the saddle and bridle inside.

"You'll get ye another horse, Jesse, and that saddle and bridle will be ready and waitin fer ye," Will said.

Jesse walked away not saying anything to Will. His tall, slender figure disappeared into the dusk.

"Papa, Jesse is walking away. Should we go after him, Papa?" Libby asked.

"Jesse will be all right, Libby. He can take care of himself. We will just let him be while he reckons with the loss of his Maggie."

Libby was inside the wagon in her bed when she heard Jesse's sobs from his bedroll under the wagon. They were deep and sorrowful sobs. Libby knew she would forever remember how her big, strong brother mourned the loss of his Maggie. Another thing she knew was that she would do everything she could to help Jesse be happy again.

***

When morning came Libby heard voices outside the wagon. It was Papa talking to Captain Jamison.

"I will be much obliged, Captain, if you could lend us your mare. A man on foot doesn't have much chance to chase the critters when they decide to go their own way. Jesse is on foot this morning since he lost Maggie."

"Yes, and I am sorry this has happened. I have had a talk with Alvin Martin and he has agreed to have his boy, Charlie, walk along behind the train and help with the livestock. I think a bit of eating dust at the back of the train should give him a better understanding of how he needs to behave on this train. Truth be told, a day of trailing the livestock will make anybody tired enough to just crawl into a bedroll at night without getting into trouble."

Libby hurried into her dress and quickly brushed her hair. She smiled as she thought about the good news that Jesse would be able to borrow Captain Jamison's mare. He wouldn't have to run on foot after the strays when he herded their cattle. She hurried through breakfast and helped Ben into the wagon. She helped Mama and Nancy pack up things away. "I heard Captain Jamison tell Papa that Jesse could borrow his mare to herd the cattle. I'll bet that will be good news for him," said Libby as she and Nancy got their bonnets from the wagon and tied them on.

"That is good news, Libby, but I expect Jesse will be sad for some time to come. He loved Maggie and riding Captain Jamison's mare will not be the same," Nancy answered.

I just wish I knew how to help Jesse," said Libby.

"I have an idea," said Nancy. "I think we can make Jesse a leather jacket. What we need is some tanned deer hide and the only way we can get that is from the Indians. They may come around to trade again. Maybe we can talk to Redtop and get him to help us. He knows the Indian talk and about their ways."

"What do you think we can trade to the Indians?" asked Libby.

"Tonight when we stop and camp we will look to see what we can find," said Nancy"

The girls followed along beside the big blue wagon as it rolled out onto the trail.

***

At noon the wagons stopped for a quick meal and there was spring water for the animals. Jesse came up from the back of the train covered with dust from his battered felt hat to his worn leather boots. He shook out his shirt collar to let the dust blow away from his neck. Dust covered his face and only his eyes were free of the fine gray dirt.He sat down by the wagon with a sigh.

"Those critters were pretty ornery this morning Jesse?"

Papa asked.

Jesse didn't speak but nodded his head, his sad face under the dust didn't have even a hint of a smile.

Libby ran to the wagon and got a washpan and filled it with water from the water barrel. She got a clean towel and some soap from the wagon and took it to Jesse. "You might want to wash your face and hands, Jesse," she said.

Jesse sat still looking at the pan of water that Libby had placed on the ground beside him. Finally he said, "Thanks Libby," and placed the pan of water between his knees and dipped his hands into the water and splashed it on his face.

"Captain Jamison says you can borrow his mare Princess. He doesn't need her right now and he is willing to let you ride her to herd our cattle," Papa said. "Think that's better than on foot, son?"

Jesse's lips twitched with a small smile and he nodded his head and said softly, "Yep."

When the wagons camped for the night and supper was cooked, dishes washed and put away Nancy, Libby and Mama went inside the big blue wagon to find something that might be traded for a deer skin. They wanted to have enough to make a jacket with fringe like the one Captain Jamison wore.

Libby looked through her scrap bag hanging on the wagon bow and took out her quilt blocks. She had six blocks finished. She needed three more to make a square. If she made the three blocks she could put them together and make a small quilt. It would be big enough for a doll quilt. Maybe the Indians would like it. It would be pretty with a back and a binding around the outside. She gathered the pieces and waited for Mama and Nancy to finish their search.

"What did you find Libby?" Mama asked.

"I have my quilt blocks and if I make three more I can make a small quilt. It is pretty with all the bright colors. I could hurry and finish three more blocks."

"That would be a good trading piece. I will help you finish it when you get your blocks done. I have found a wool blanket that I saved for our new home," Mama said and smoothed a grey blanket with bright stripes at the edges and laid it across her arm. "The Indians need blankets and we can make another quilt to take the place of this."

Nancy held up a beautiful appliqued quilt with red roses twining across a white background. "This is something Grandma gave me for my wedding day. I have always loved it but I am going to trade it because of Jesse."

Mama asked, "Are you sure you want to give it up? Grandma spent many hours sewing that for you and you may want to have it for your own home. Grandma is not here to make you another one."

"Yes, I will give it up. It is the best thing I have to trade and I want to help Jesse," Nancy said and stroked the quilt that lay across her knees as she sat on her bed.

"Lets put these things into two pillow cases and slide them under your bed Nancy," Mama said. "Libby, better keep your scrap bag handy and get started on your next block right away. I will ask Papa to talk to Redtop about finding Indians who will want to trade. Now off to bed. We will be up early in the morning."

The quilt and blanket were put away and Mama left the wagon to go to the tent.

"I wish I could light the lantern and stay up and sew awhile," Libby said. "I need to hurry and get this finished."

"Better turn in now. The light isn't that good for sewing and tomorrow you can ride in the wagon and work on it. I'll walk with Mama and look for wood for cooking fires," answered Nancy.

The next day, the wagon squeaked and rumbled over the

rough ground, bouncing Libby up and down on her bed. She was hot and thirsty and she could smell the dust as it swirled around outside.

"I'll get this done yet," she called out to no one but herself.

With a determined jerk she spread out the small quilt and smoothed it across her lap. She looked for her needle but it had dropped into her lap. She picked up the thread end and the needle, pursed her lips in a tight line around the thread, and once more threaded it. She braced her feet against the floor of the wagon to keep from rocking from side to side. Then she slowly stitched the last piece, smoothed the quilt out on her lap on the wrong side and examined her stitches.

"That's done," she said and puffed out her breath in relief.

She put her things away in her sewing bag and when the wagon slowed to a stop, quickly climbed down and ran to tell Nancy and Mama her good news.

"Mama, Nancy, I finished stitching my quilt. It's done and ready to bind. I got it finished in time to trade if you will help me with the binding and backing, Mama"

"We can work on it tonight after we finish our meal," Mama said.

"I'm anxious to hear what Redtop says about trading with the Indians," said Nancy.

"Papa will let us know tonight if he has had a chance to talk to him. Let's get things ready for trading in case we meet some Indians soon," Mama said.

***

The supper fire had burned down to bright, red coals that glowed in the darkness surrounding the Campbell's camp. Papa and Jesse sat on oxen yokes resting. The sound of a harmonica came from a across the circle of wagons. A light breeze blew against the red coals of the supper fire, sending bright sparks up into the sky.

Libby could hardly wait to find out if Papa had talked to Redtop about trading with the Indians. She whirled around and called out, "Papa?"

"Libby, let Papa rest. We must finish our chores and then we can talk to him" Mama said.

Jesse stood and stretched his arms above his head. "I'll take a little walk and stretch my legs a bit," he said and walked outside the circle of light.

Papa said, "Come girls. I have some news for you."

Libby and Nancy hurried to sit beside Papa..

"I spoke to Redtop today about getting a tanned deer skin from the Indians. He thinks that it would be best to wait until we get to Ft Laramie. There will be a lot of traders there and more than likely some Indians wanting to trade their skins. I think he is right. I would wait until we reach the fort where you will have a better chance to find a good deer skin."

"But Papa, isn't Ft. Laramie a long way from here? It will take so long to ever get there."

"Be patient Libby. We will see Chimney Rock in a few days, and when we pass by there,
it won't be long before we reach Ft. Laramie. I think that's the best plan girls."

" I am sure Redtop is right," said Nancy. "We will make sure we are ready for trading. "

"Off to bed now girls. If we have good traveling we should reach Ft. Laramie before very long," Papa said.

CHIMNEY ROCK

All day the wagons traveled over the hot, dusty trail. Libby wiped her face with the back of her hand and then looked at the grime that covered it . She wondered how much further they would go before they stopped. She felt as though she could not walk one step further when she heard a yell. It was Jesse who came riding up from behind the wagons where he had been herding cattle.

" Ya-hoo! Chimney Rock. Look way beyond that big lump ahead. See the chimney?" he yelled.

Libby looked ahead and saw a big mound of rock in the distance. "Where, Jesse? Where do you see a chimney? That looks like a big mountain of rock to me."

"Oh, that's Court House Rock. We'll be going by it today. See how it looks like a real court house and beside it is Jail House Rock. The closer we get the more it will look like a real court house."

"But you said you could see Chimney Rock. Where is it?" Libby asked as she squinted her eyes in the bright sun.

" It's beyond Court House Rock. See that finger sticking up toward the sky. It's little now but as we get closer it will get bigger and look higher. Captain Jamison says it is more that three hundred feet tall."

Libby hurried to Mama and Nancy. "Look," she shouted. Look ahead. That's Court House Rock and Jail House Rock. Beyond it is Chimney Rock. It looks little now but when we get closer it will look much bigger. Captain Jamison told Jesse so."

"That means we are not far from Ft. Laramie, " Nancy shouted and clapped her hands.

Mama smiled and said, "Make sure you have everything you plan to trade in good condition and all together."

***

Somehow the dust wasn't so thick and the flies and mosquitoes were not pesky at all. Libby was so excited that she moved along quickly. She used her hands to shade her eyes and looked at Chimney Rock which was still small against the blue sky.

There was nooning, then the long afternoon hours began to seem endless. Libby called out to Liza as she saw their wagon pass by. "Liza. Do you see Chimney Rock? It's way, way ahead but we are getting closer all the time."

Liza jumped down from from the wagon when it slowed. "Where Libby? I don't see it," she shouted as she ran toward

Libby.

Libby pointed ahead and stood looking at the small spire reaching up into the blue sky.

“Whoops Libby,” Liza said. “We better get a going. Look where the wagons are and we are way behind.”

The girls ran along the trail jumping over sagebrush and running around cactus until they had reached their wagons again.

“Libby, let’s pull off some of these Prickly Pear blooms and make a bouquet for Star. We can put them in a tin cup or a bowl. ”

“Well, I like sunflowers better but I’ll help you. ”

The girls reached down for the beautiful yellow flowers, being ever so careful to avoid the stickers of the Prickly Pear plant.

“Ouch,” yelled Liza. This plant is wicked. I just stuck myself good and when I tried to get away I got a dozen little tiny stickers in my hand. Let’s stop. I have three blooms. How many do you have?”

“I have two. This should be enough for a cup full. If your Mama will let you use one of her tin cups it will look pretty.”

"I know she will let me use mine. I can carry them in my apron back to our wagon."

"Their yellow, waxy petals look almost like a rose. They are so pretty. I guess the bees think so because they are buzzing around you."

"I better get away from the pesky bees and put them in the wagon. After supper I'll bring them and show you and I will bring Star too." Liza ran toward her wagon making the dust fly from behind her high topped brown shoes.

The wagons rolled past a Sioux Indian village. There were many tepees made of skins pulled around tall poles. The poles reached above to small smoke holes at the top. Some tepees were decorated with drawings of animals and figures.

Libby watched children running about and women cooking over outdoor fires. Some Indian men were leading horses to a corral and others sat beside fires.

The Indian children watched as the wagon train rolled past. The girls wore deerskin dresses and the boys wore leather breechclouts, extending from their waist and hanging down like an apron to cover the front of their bodies. They stared at Libby and the other women in their long dresses and sun bonnets as they walked by. Some would run behind the tepees to hide, lean around them to stare, then giggle and hide again.

Libby pulled at her skirt and brushed the dust from her face. She felt strange to be the one who was different. She straightened her shoulders and lifted her head high. She stamped her high topped shoes up and down, determined to show these Indians. Why were they laughing? She would show them that a pioneer girl could walk and walk fast.

***

When the wagons pulled off the trail to camp for the night, there were excited voices as the travelers looked across the prairie at the huge mound across from the campsite. They had reached Courthouse Rock and many people from the wagon train were going across the prairie for a closer look.

The supper was cooked, animals watered, and dishes were put away. Libby was excited about the big rock looming up on the prairie. She wanted to get close and maybe write her name on it, like many travelers had done before.

"Mama, may I go see the rock?" she asked.

"Libby, it may look very close but it is quite a distance there and back. You wouldn't be able to walk there and you have no horse to ride.

"But Mama, I can walk that far. I walk that far every day

right beside the wagons," Libby pleaded.

"You will need to stay here and take care of Ben. He is much too small to walk that far," Mama answered.

Libby was disappointed. She wanted to change her mother's decision.

"Mama, Jesse and Nancy and you and Papa are going and if everyone else is going, why can't I go too?"

"Enough Libby. You are not to leave the campsite, remember? When we reach Ft Laramie your punishment will be fulfilled and you can then, hopefully, remember rules we must all obey when we travel with this train. Ben will need you to take good care of him while we are away. Stay close to the wagon and you will be safe."

Libby sat down on the wagon tongue and propped her elbows on her knees covering her dusty face with her hands. She didn't want Mama to see her tears that came so quickly.

I am always the one left out she thought. Everybody but me gets to do things. Maybe I just don't belong to this family. Maybe I am just an outsider and came from somewhere else.

Sobs came and as hard as she tried, they wouldn't stop.

Mama turned and put her hands on her hips and stared at

Libby. "Young lady," she said. "Enough of that feeling sorry for yourself. You know that you are being punished for putting us all in danger of the Indians. Straighten up and accept it and finish it with good grace. We will be back before dark. You and Ben can play inside the wagon while we are away."

Libby stood up and brushed her cheeks. They felt muddy and stung from the salty tears. She took the washpan and poured a small bit of water from the water barrel into it and washed her face and dusty hands.

"I'll take good care of Ben, Mama."

Shadows crept around the wagons. Papa rode Toby, one of the mules, up to the supper fire. Mama climbed up behind Papa and followed Jesse on the Captain's horse and Nancy behind Mason Connors on his horse.

Libby sat on the wagon tongue and held Little Ben's hand. They moved their feet back and forth in the dust and watched nervously as the riders rode away from the camp.

"I'm not afraid Ben. We are safe as can be. Liza is going to bring Star over in a little while. You will want to see Star won't you?" asked Libby.

Little Ben bowed his head and sniffled as he rubbed his eyes with his fist. "I want Mama and Papa," he cried.

" Don't you worry. They will be back before dark. We can go inside the wagon and I'll read you a story."

She lifted the little boy and helped him climb into the wagon. She took a book from its safe place under her bed and with Ben beside her she began to read. Ben snuggled against her and it wasn't long before his sleepy head nodded up and down. Libby put the book away and settled the little boy on her bed for a nap.

She climbed out of the wagon and stood listening to the sound of insects as they called out in the evening air. A breeze blew around the wagon and cooled her face. She looked out toward Court House Rock but could no longer see her family on horseback.

She spoke to herself. "Guess they are there by now."

She reached for crackers Mama had slipped into her pocket after supper. She sat down on the wagon tongue and ate the treat. She crossed her fingers and wished.

"I will never be left out again."

She sat wishing and wishing until the shadows grew dark and the lantern light glowed through the wagon covers around the circle. Libby could smell the frying meat and the smoke from the supper fires and hear the voices of children. It would soon be dark and bedtime.

"Lib-bee".

That was Lizzie's voice. Libby knew it at once.

"Here, Lizzie," Libby called out.

Lizzie came running through the shadows carrying a small box in her hands. She hurried to Libby and held out the small box.

"See," she puffed from her run. "See how pretty Star looks with the yellow flowers?"

"She is so pretty," Libby answered. "The yellow flowers set off her braids that you made for her. She needs a headband and a feather in it and she would look like an Indian girl."

"Well, do you have something to make one for her, Libby?"

"Only my blue ribbons. We might find a feather from a bird somewhere. I may have one in my bag of possibles. Let's go look."

Ben was still asleep on Libby's bed so the girls knelt on the floor of the wagon while Libby opened a drawstring bag she had sewn from scraps. There was the pretty rock she had found at the beginning of their trip, there were some seed pods she had picked along the trail, some dried flowers and a scrap of red cloth, a wooden whistle Jesse had made for her and two black and white feathers—one was tiny and one was as long as her middle finger.

"We can use the tiny one, Liza, and we can use this scrap of red cloth if we fold it just right so the raw edges won't show."

Libby laid the feather and red cloth aside then quickly stuffed the other things back into the bag.

The girls worked, smoothing the cloth then pressing it between their fingers to the right width for Star's head. Liza put the cloth around the doll's head and tied it in the back. Libby slipped the tiny black and white feather under the head-band.

They put the doll back in the box with the yellow flowers and smiled as they admired their Indian doll beside the beautiful waxy, yellow flowers.

"Oh, I want Ben to see her," Libby said. She gently patted the boy's shoulder and he rolled over and stared at the girls as he called out.

"Libby, Where is Mama?"

"Mama will be back soon," Libby answered. "I want you to see Star. Lizzie and I made her into an Indian doll. Look at her headband. See the feather we put under it just like a real Indian girl might do."

Little Ben sat up and rubbed his eyes then bent down to look at the doll that Lizzie held out to him. He laughed as he reached out to touch the feather gently with the tip of his finger.

"Just look Ben," she said. "Look at how pretty she is."

Ben laughed and pulled his arms back from the doll. "Indian doll," he said.

Liza stood up and looked out the back of the wagon. "Oh, it's dark outside. I have to go. Will you walk part way with me, Libby?"

"Come on Ben. We will walk to the end of our wagon with Liza just far enough that she can see her wagon."

Holding tight to Ben's hand Libby climbed out of the back of the wagon behind Lizzie. As they walked toward the front of the wagon a dark figure ran out from the front of the wagon toward the open plain. The girls stared at the tall figure as he slipped silently away in moccasined feet. He carried a spear and the feathers on his head were outlined in the dusky last light of day.

"Indian," shouted Little Ben.

Libby quickly clamped her hand over Little Ben's mouth."

"Run, Libby, run," whispered Liza.

Pulling Little Ben beside her Libby raced behind Liza toward Liza's wagon. The ground was rough and Little Ben stumbled and started to cry. He pulled away from Libby's hand and sat down on the ground. "Ouch, ouch. My foot hurts," he cried out.

Libby wanted to run and get away from the Indian. She was afraid he might come back but she leaned down and helped Ben climb onto her back. She had to help her brother. He had stepped on a prickly pear with his bare feet.

"Liza run fast. Run home. Tell your Papa about the Indian. Hurry."

Libby stumbled back toward the wagon carrying Little Ben on her back. Just as she reached the wagon, she heard the sound of horses' hooves not far away. Quickly she helped Ben into the wagon and climbed in beside him. She put him on her bed and patted him on the back whispering in his ear. "Shush,

Ben. Indians might be near."

They sat on the bed as quiet as they could. There was no sound outside except the the approaching horses and a loud snort as they reached the circle of wagons.

"Libby, we are home," called Mama.

She put her head in the wagon's pucker hole and looked inside the dark wagon.

"Libby, whatever is wrong? Why haven't you lit the lantern?"

"Indian," called Little Ben. "We saw Indian."

Papa reached inside the wagon and took the lantern and lit it.

"What about an Indian, Ben?"

"Oh, Papa," Libby answered. "We did see an Indian. He was just outside by the front of the wagon when we started to walk Liza toward home. He ran fast out to the open prairie. It was all most dark and we could't see where he went but he wore moccasins and carried a spear with feathers. We were scared and started to run with Liza to her wagon but Ben stepped on a prickly pear and I carried him back to our wagon. We were so scared."

"Don't you worry. I'll get the men to help scout out the camp and see if we find him. Jesse will stay here with you and keep his gun ready. Don't cry now and stay inside the wagon. Jesse will be just outside."

The men came running from their wagons carrying their rifles and pistols. They called out in shouts as they searched around the wagons.

Libby looked out the pucker hole of the wagon and watched as lanterns bobbed up and down around the wagons. Dogs barked and the men shouted.

"No Indians here! He has gone!

"All is well. It is safe folks," called Captain Jamison.

Mama sat down on the bed beside Ben.

"Let me see your feet Ben. You may need some stickers taken out."

Ben lay on his back and stretched out his leg. Mama took one of his feet in her hand. "Bring the light Libby. His foot is full of stickers.

Libby held the lantern close and mama used tweezers to pull the tiny stickers out of the bottom of Ben's feet. When Mama finished, she covered the bottoms of Ben's feet with salve and then pulled on clean socks over his sore feet.

"Now, that will make you feel better my boy," she said.

Libby got the washpan and poured some water into it from the water barrel. She washed her feet and dried them on an old towel.

"Better let me check you for stickers Libby," Mama said.

Libby lifted her legs placing her feet in Mama's lap.

"I can see a few that need to come out." Mama carefully gripped the stickers with the tweezers then pulled them out. She smoothed her fingers over the bottoms of Libby's feet

"Feel anymore stickers Libby?"

"No, Mama, I think that is all. Thank you for pulling them out.

"Then it's bed time. You can snuggle up on your bed with Ben while I make sure Papa and Jesse and Nancy are alright."

"Did you have a good time Mama? Were there many names on the rock?"

"Oh there were thousands of names. But guess what? Papa and Jesse carved all our names on the rock. Yours and Ben's too. And Mason Connors drew a box and inside he wrote his name and below it he wrote Nancy's name."

"What does that mean, Mama? Nancy isn't in Mason Connor's family."

"Maybe he just wants her to be in his family. We will see."

Libby lay awake in her bed listening to Ben's soft breathing. She heard voices outside as people walked to their wagons. She thought about Nancy. Would she marry Mason Connors and leave their family? She hoped not. She didn't want her big sister to go away. If she married Mason Connors she might go far away once they reached Oregon. Libby thought about it until she was tired and was just asleep when Mama came and carried Ben to the tent to his own bed.

The sun was bright when libby heard Mama and Nancy rattling the pots in the grub box. Nancy stuck her head inside the wagon and called out, "Are you going to get up Sleepy Head? The day is well on its way and time for breakfast."

***

Voices came near and the riders soon came back to the wagons. Mama came to the wagon and Libby climbed down to meet her.

"Did you have a good time Mama? Were there many names on the rock?"

"Oh there were thousands of names. But guess what, Papa and Jesse carved all our names on the rock. Yours and Ben's too. And Mason Connors drew a box and inside he wrote his name and below it he wrote Nancy's name."

"What does that mean, Mama? Nancy isn't in Mason Connor's family."

"Maybe he just wants her to be in his family. We will see."

Libby lay awake in her bed listening to Ben's soft breathing. She thought about Nancy. Would she marry Mason Connors and leave their family. She didn't want her big sister to go away. Libby thought about it until Mama came and carried Ben to the tent to his own bed.

***

The sun was bright when Libby heard Mama and Nancy rattling the pots in the grub box.

Nancy stuck her head inside the wagon and called, "Are you going to get up Sleepy Head? It's time for breakfast."

Libby helped with breakfast then washed and packed away the dishes. The wagons moved out and Libby walked away from the line of wagons far enough to escape the worst of the dust. She could see Chimney Rock ahead. It looked close but at the nooning Pa said that it would be evening before they reached it.

. It was late afternoon when the wagon train rolled by Chimney Rock. Its tall chimney rose up in the air several hundred feet. At the bottom, the rock base spread out in a wide platform that anchored the tall peak.

The wagons camped across from the sand chimney. Some of the people were going across to visit it. Libby knew that she wasn't allowed to leave the wagon train and she sat on the wagon tongue with a sad look as she stared out at the giant chimney.

Papa and Jessie stood near the wagon talking.

"That is a mighty tall chimney if ever I saw one," Papa said.

"I want to ride over to see it up close, Papa," Jessie said.

I figured you would want to. Did you check with Mr. Jamison about riding his horse?"

" I won't need to. Nancy and Mason are going and Mason said I could ride one of their horses.'

" Fine then," Papa said. "Mama and I will stay here this time. That Indian that has been coming around may show up again."

"Hey, Libby. What you so sad about?" Jesse asked. "We're at Chimney Rock and it won't be long before we reach Fort Laramie. You'll soon be free again," Jessie said.

"Guess so," Libby mumbled. "Maybe I'll be just like everybody else and can come and go like the rest of the family."

"Yes, you can daughter. I hope you will think about where you go when we reach the fort. We need to be careful. This is dangerous country. But I know you can do it," Papa said and came over to Libby and reached his big hand out to touch her cheek.

FORT LARAMIE

The wagons rumbled past Fort Laramie where many Indian tepees rose up around it. Indians and people from other wagon trains all rushed about outside the fort. The wagon train moved on past the busy fort toward the Laramie river and made camp. It was evening and time for supper.

Libby and Nancy hurried to get things out of the grub box and Jesse made a fire and hung up Mama's big cooking pot under the metal tripod.

"The fort is an exciting place with all the Indians and traders there. It was so noisy I could hardly hear what anyone said. Mama, are we going to the fort tonight?" Nancy asked.

" I think it best to wait until morning. We can have a clear view of the place in daylight and you girls can get Redtop to help you trade."

"You can be sure Redtop wants to visit his old trapper friends tonight and have a little fun. He has been guiding the wagon train for a long time and needs to kick up his heels a little," Jesse said.

Libby waited to hear someone mention that her punishment was over now that they had reached Fort Laramie but everyone was too excited about finally reaching the fort. Papa and Jesse talked about fixing the wagon wheels, Mama and Nancy talked about shopping for some supplies and Will said he wanted to ride back to the fort to see some old friends who would be there to trade with the Indians.

After supper Libby sat with the family around the camp fire. There was excited talk about Fort Laramie. Libby smiled a secret smile. Maybe it wasn't even important to anyone else but she knew that at last her punishment was over. She would no longer have to stick close to the wagon. She would be able to go with Mama and Nancy to the fort.

The next morning the wagon bumped along as the big mules pulled it toward Fort Laramie. Libby, Nancy, and Mama sat on the girls' beds holding tight to the wooden bows to keep from sliding as the wagon wheels ran over bumps and dipped down into holes. Jesse, Papa and Little Ben sat on the wagon seat in front and Papa called out to the mules.

"Getty-up Toby. Get along Tucker," he shouted over the jangling harness and rumbling wheels urging the mules to a trot as they came riding up toward the high adobe walls of the fort.

"We may have been on the trail more than six hundred

miles but these mules can show that we are no slackers. The Campbells haven't had all their pride whipped out of 'em," Jesse yelled out.

"Yep, you are right, son. We still have a little sassafras left in us. We can show off these high stepping mules a little," Papa said and laughed and so did everyone else.

There were many tepees outside the fort walls and many other wagons of immigrant families stopped outside the fort as well. The families walked among the Indians looking at the goods they had for sale.

Papa pulled back on the reins and stopped the mules, leaving the wagon far back from the Indian tepees.

"Jessie," he said, "Let's get that wagon wheel fixed and then you can look at the sights. Girls, Redtop said he would be outside watching for you and would help you make your trade. Let's all meet at the wagon when our trading is done."

Libby climbed down from the wagon behind Mama and Nancy. They walked past tepees of Indian families who had their trade goods spread out on top of buffalo robes. There were children and dogs dashing back and forth around the tepees. Libby wanted to stop and look at the goods but Mama and Nancy hurried past and Libby had to run to catch up.

A tall man came toward them and asked, “May I help you Ma’am?”

“Yes sir,” answered Nancy. “We are looking for our wagon scout. His name is Redtop and his hair is just as his name says, red.”

“I know the man and you will find him just beyond the corner of the fort with a group of scouts and mountain men. He is probably swapping stories with his friends.”

Libby followed Mama and Nancy. They soon saw Redtop bent at the waist throwing colored stones upon a deer skin. There was loud laughter as Redtop raked up all the stones.

“Ah, haw!” a man called out. “You cleaned up good all right, Redtop. Now give me a chance to win some back,” he said as Redtop exchanged his stones for gun powder.

“You see them circles on that skin? I put every stone inside the first circle. You can’t even get yours into the last circle. When you have had time to practice I’ll wager you again. Right now I have some ladies who need my help; keep your powder dry partner,” Redtop answered.

“Ladies, lets get over to Red Willow’s tepee. He has the best skins around. More than likely he will take a likin to what you have there. Nancy took out the wedding quilt, the blanket and

Libby's pieced baby quilt. Mama held out a round pin holder with two needles in it and asked, "Do you think this will get us maybe two nice deer skins, Redtop?"

"It should. Lets head out to find Red Willow. He is just around the corner.

They reached Red Willow's tepee and found beautiful beaded moccasins, leggings, and buffalo robes spread out in front of his tepee. He sat in front of the tepee while his wife Morning Dove sat just inside. Redtop spoke in the Sioux language to the tall Indian dressed in beautiful beaded leggings and shirt. His dark braids hung down over his shoulders.

Red Willow turned and pointed to Morning Dove who stood up showing her long leather dress fringed on the sleeves and at the bottom. She wore a beaded headband around her forehead, and one large braid hung down her back. She smiled then turned and bent her head and disappeared into the tepee. When she returned she carried a bundle of tanned deerskins which she spread out on a buffalo robe.

Redtop motioned to Nancy. "Put your things on the robe beside the deerskins," he said.

Nancy spread the beautiful wedding quilt out then lay out Libby's small quilt and Mama's blanket. The sun spread over them, making the colors bright and beautiful.

"Hump," Red Willow said, and Morning Dove smiled a wide smile.

Redtop spoke to Red Willow again in his language. After much talk back and forth, Redtop picked up two golden deer skins and lifted them high.

"How do these suit you ladies? I don't think you could find nicer skins anywhere around here. Morning Star can't be beat when it comes to tanning skins," he said.

Nancy, Mama, and then Libby reached out and smoothed the skins between their palms then Mama held one of the skins up, measuring by touching it to her nose and extending the other side to the length of her arm.

"These are nice, " she said. "But we may need another skin to be sure we have enough for fringe."

Redtop bent over and started patting the quilts and blankets while talking in the Sioux language to Red Willow. All the while Red Willow kept shaking his head.

"No!" he said, so loud it surprised Morning Dove and she went inside the tepee.

Mama reached quickly into her apron pocket drawing out

the little pin holder with the needles. She handed them to Redtop and said, "Maybe these will help."

Redtop took the needles to Red Willow and lay them in the palm of his hand. "Trade now?" he asked.

Red Willow bent his chin to his chest then nodded up and down and answered, "trade now."

Redtop gathered up the two deer skins then picked up another one of the same color and softness and laid them in Nancy's arms. "You did yourself proud there Miss. That will make a fine jacket." he said.

Mama took off her apron and rolled the deer skins in it and covered them completely. "Jesse will never see these skins or have any idea we got them. Now lets go inside the fort to check for mail and get a few supplies."

Inside the supply store Libby looked at the tall shelves behind the counter where boxes, bags and jars of food were stored. A clerk behind the counter waited on customers who asked for sugar, meal, flour, and coffee. As the customers walked away they could be heard grumbling.

"These prices are far too high."

" We can't afford this."

" Our money will soon be gone."

When their turn came, Mama stepped up to the counter with Nancy and Libby close behind her. "Our name is Campbell. Would there be any mail for us?" Mama asked.

The clerk reached under the counter and pulled out a large reed basket and placed it on the counter. "Look for yourself, ma'am," then went to help the next customer.

Nancy and Libby quickly thumbed through the letters and pieces of paper, cards and small pieces of rawhide with writing on them. There was dust and a few small pebbles at the bottom of the basket. Libby felt her fingers getting dusty but kept looking at each piece. Nancy made a stack of mail on the counter. They were determined to find any mail that might belong to the Campbell family. Near the bottom of the basket Libby saw a letter with Grandma's beautiful handwriting with its little curls and full letters. She picked up the letter and held it under the light. It was addressed to her, Miss Elizabeth Ann Campbell, Care of Ft Laramie.

"It's for me," Libby screamed and jumped up and down waving the letter in the air.

"Put it in your pocket and you can read it when we get to the wagon," Mama said. "We have to get our supplies now."

Are there any more letters for us, girls?" Mama asked.

"That's everything Mama," answered Nancy. "We have looked carefully."

"Can I get you anything, ma'am?" the clerk asked.

"Yes, I need five pounds of meal and a pound of coffee and a handful of those potatoes in the barrel, Mama said.

The clerk gathered the things together and set them on the counter. That will be five dollars and twenty-five cents," the clerk said.

Mama stood silent for a moment resting both hands on the counter. Her eyes were wide and her face turned pale.

The busy clerk spoke loud enough for everyone to hear.

"Well, take it or leave it. I don't have time to spare here."

Mama pulled open the strings on her little velvet purse and reached for the money inside. Counting carefully, she reached out to the clerk and gave it to him.

"Thank yea Ma'am," he said then turned to the next customer.

Gathering up the supplies Mama, Nancy and Libby walked outside the fort's gate into the warm sun.

“Are you all right, Mama?” asked Nancy. “You’re so pale.”

“Yes, I’m fine. It was a shock to hear that man charge so much for supplies. At this rate we will have to be very careful and make do with what we have and what we can get along the trail.”

***

When they returned to their campsite dusk was settling in around the wagons. Libby sat down on the wagon tongue and carefully drew out Grandma’s letter from her pocket. Everyone gathered around as she tore open the end of the envelope. She pulled out the folded pages inside. As they slid out, something fell into her lap. She looked down and there was a tiny red ribbon bow around some soft grey fur.

“Read it Libby. We want to know what Grandma says, ” Mama said.

Libby opened the pages and began Grandma’s letter.

> Dear Libby,
>
> I hope you will enjoy this little bit
> of fur from Greyboy’s thick coat.
> He is very well and purrs by the

> fire at night to keep Grandpa and me company. I know he misses you but perhaps this little reminder will keep him near. We miss you and hope all of you are well. Love, Grandma.

Libby laid the first page in her lap with the bit of fur. She stroked the fur thinking of her cat and wishing she could hear him purring by her side.

"Read Libby. What else does Grandma say?" Nancy asked.

Libby opened the second page of the letter and began to read.

> Dear Family,
>
> We have missed you all so very much. The summer has been a hot one but Grandpa has kept the garden hoed and watered and we had a good stand of vegetables this year. I have canned pickles,

green beans, tomatoes and some jars of relish too.

I hope you have had good luck traveling and your supplies are holding out and your animals are staying healthy. We have a new calf from our milk cow Bonnie. She is the prettiest little calf. I know Ben would like to pet her. Our neighbor, John Hess, is putting up the hay. The barn is full and we have two big hay stacks. There will be plenty for winter. John's children, Claude, Bessie and Alice asked about you all. They came with John for the haying. Grandpa and I are well and doing our daily walks past the pond and around our front pasture. When we come home I make supper for us and Grandpa reads the daily Bible verses. Our nightly prayers ask for your safe-

keeping. Send a letter when you
can. Love to all, Grandma

Libby closed the family letter and gave it to Mama. She carefully put her letter, along with the precious puff of hair, into the envelope, opened her possibles bag, and placed it inside. She would write a letter to Grandma and hope for a chance to send it with someone returning to Missouri.

For supper that night there was buffalo stew, corn bread and best of all, boiled potatoes.

"I just about forgot how potatoes tasted," Libby said as she scraped the last bit from her plate.

JESSE'S JACKET

After supper Nancy and Libby carefully unwrapped the three deer skins from Mama's apron, folded them, and put them under the covers at the bottom of Nancy's bed.

Nancy patted the bed and whispered to Libby, "These are safe and we will just be careful when we work on them that we keep our secret," she said.

"When will we start the jacket Nancy?" asked Libby.

"We will be traveling tomorrow morning and we can start planning then. We may get some help from Mrs. Jamison the Captain's wife. She made his beautiful leather jacket."

The wagons rolled onto the trail as the morning sky was turning pink. Ft Laramie was soon left behind. The noise of clanging metal, barking dogs and the shouts and loud voices were now gone. The oxen faithfully plodded over the trail.

Libby, Mama, and Nancy walked beside the family wagon. It was the day for the Campbell wagons to be first in line and there was not much dust around them. They talked about the jacket they would make for Jesse.

"I think it should be rather plain with fringe just along the length of the sleeves," said Nancy.

"Yes, Jesse isn't fond of a lot of fuss and feathers," Mama said.

"How will we know how big to make it?" asked Libby.

"Oh, we can use one of Jesse's shirts to measure the sleeve length and the width of the shoulders," Mama answered. We will have plenty of time. We will get a pattern made by the time we reach the Sweetwater River and Devil's Gate."

The wagons traveled over a rough trail that climbed up higher, making the mules and oxen slow as they struggled to pull their heavy load. By the nooning the animals and their masters were ready for a rest.

Libby ate her cold beans and spoke softly, more to herself than to the rest of the family. "Beans, beans, beans. All we ever eat is beans."

"Young lady," Mama said, "You may very well be glad to have a few beans before we get to Oregon."

"Yea! I'll take your share of beans if you don't want 'em," Jesse said. "Seems like I never get enough beans or anything else. My old stomach can sure use any you don't want." He leaned back his head and laughed until his hat rolled off his head and down behind his back to the ground.

" Here, Jesse. I am full to the brim and I don't need this piece of cornbread. You take it," said Nancy and handed it to Jesse.

"Thanks, Nancy. It'll sure taste good to me," Jesse said.

Libby sat on the dusty ground and bent her head forward until her chin rested on her chest. She felt ashamed that she had complained about the beans. She hurried to help clean up the dishes and as she walked with Mama to the wagon she whispered, "I am sorry Mama."

"Libby, the beans get real monotonous I know but we are lucky to have them. Some people are already low on supplies. How they will make it on to Oregon I don't know."

"I won't complain, Mama," said Libby. "I know that it's not the same as home. Sometimes I just get tired. I get tired of walking in the dust, the same food so often, the hot sun and just feeling dusty and dirty so much of the time."

Mama reached over and put her arm around Libby's waist and pulled her close. "Me too. Me too," she said and laughed her tinkling laugh that floated over Libby's head and made Libby laugh too.

At the end of the day they found a camping spot near a

good spring with plenty of fresh water. Jesse and Libby took buckets of water to the oxen and then washed the dust from their faces and noses.

"That should feel better now," she said as she finished the last one.

"They can breathe better now," said Jesse. I never thought I would need to wash the oxen's faces but they deserve a cool off after this rocky dusty road. I hope we reach the Sweetwater soon. These fellows need a good bath"

***

The evening camp was quiet except for a few barking dogs and the lonesome song from a mouth organ somewhere in the distance. Supper was finished and dishes put away. Papa and Jesse sat by the smoldering, red coals of the supper fire, resting their backs against the ox yolks. Mr. Stampers sat nearby with his knees drawn up and encircled with his long arms. The low rumble of their voices trailed after Mama, Libby and Nancy as they walked toward Captain Jamison's wagon. Mrs. Jamison had promised to help them make a pattern for Jesse's leather jacket. Mama carried the deerskins and one of Jesse's old shirts that had holes worn in both elbows.

"I hope Mrs. Jamison will know how to help us with this,"

Nancy said.

"More than likely she has made more than one jacket," Mama answered.

"Captain Jamison has a really grand jacket, doesn't he?" Libby asked.

"Yes, Mrs Jamison made it for him," Nancy said.

When they reached the Jamison wagon Nancy cupped her mouth with her open hands and called, "Hello. Mrs. Jamison".

Mrs. Jamison stepped down from her wagon and said "Come in, come in. I was just making a space for the cutting. Climb on up and we'll get started."

Libby looked around the large Jamison wagon. It was bigger than their family wagon but was filled in every corner and crevice. There was a lamp, trunks, boxes, and barrels. There were rifles hanging on hooks on the bows, coiled ropes, and hooks for jackets and rain coats. Mrs. Jamison had pushed aside their feather bed leaving three wide, flat walnut boards that were used to support the feather bed.

"We can use this as a cutting table," Mrs. Jamison said. "We brought along this walnut lumber to make some furniture when we reach Oregon. Libby, you can sit on that box there and rest your legs. Nancy, you and your mother stand near and give me instructions as to how you want this jacket made."

Mama ripped the seams out of Jesse's old shirt and spread the sleeves over the boards. "Yes," said Mrs. Jamison I see we need to make the sleeves in this jacket man sized so that they will be long enough. Now let's see the deer skins. Oh yes, these are beautiful skins," she said as she spread the skins across the boards.

They worked cutting the pieces for the jacket until Libby grew so sleepy she found herself nodding off then waking with a start. Mama was rolling up the pieces they had cut and Nancy was putting the scraps in her sewing bag.

"Time to go, Libby," Mama said

"Thanks Mrs. Jamison," Nancy said as they climbed out of the wagon.

Mama echoed Nancy, "Yes, thank you, Eudora, we are much obliged."

"You are more than welcome. This will be a nice surprise for Jesse and maybe make up a little bit for his losing his mare. If you need any help, please call on me."

"Goodnight," they called one last time as they stepped down from the wagon and started back home.

***

Evenings after supper and before bedtime were now spent working on Jesse's Jacket. Nancy, Mama and Libby huddled inside the family wagon and by lantern light worked on sewing seams, fitting in sleeves and making fringe. Libby had learned to cut the fringe very carefully. It would be sewn on the jacket sleeves.

"I know Jesse is going to like this jacket," Mama said as her needle went in and out.

"A few more evenings sewing and I think it will be finished," Nancy answered.

"Careful, careful, Libby," Mama warned. "Take your time and make each piece of fringe just the same as the one before."

Libby put the scissors down and wiped her sweaty palms on the sides of her dress. She smoothed the long piece of fringe out across her bed and stood back to look at the even strips of deer hide.

"It looks nice Libby. You have done a good job," Nancy said.

"I think it's nice too but my fingers hurt from squeezing the scissors so long," Libby said.

"It's time we stopped for the night and got ready for bed. Papa and Jesse may wonder what we are up to if we don't show ourselves soon," Mama said.

Carefully the new jacket pieces were put away under Nancy's's mattress and the scraps were gathered and put into her scrap bag. Mama called goodnight and went to the sleeping tent.

INDEPENDENCE ROCK

Libby lay quietly in her bed. She could hear Nancy stirring under her covers and she called softly. "Nancy, will we soon be to Independence Rock?"

"Papa says we should reach there tomorrow," Nancy answered.

"Do you think I will get to write my name there?" Libby asked.

"Well, your punishment is over and you don't have to stay at the wagon. It is possible."

"I wish I could go with you and Mason."

"I'll ask Mason if you can ride behind me on one of Mason's horses. I know he plans to go. Of course only if Mama and Papa agree."

"Oh Nancy, would you really? That would be so much fun and I could write my name like everyone else."

"We'll see. And you know that you have to prove you are responsible and think first before you do things."

"I will Nancy. I will I will. I will be so responsible."

"All right then. Tomorrow we will ask Papa and Mama for permission and then I will ask Mason. Goodnight now Little Sis.

Libby whispered, "Good night Nancy." She lay smiling in the dark thinking of the trip to Independence Rock but before long, in spite of trying to stay awake to think about the fun, her eyes closed and she was asleep.

***

They rolled out the next morning early. Libby followed along beside the family wagon. There was trouble keeping the cattle from the ponds of alkali along the way. The cattle ran toward the ponds for a drink and the herders had to hurry to turn them away. If the cattle drank the alkali water they might die. There were skulls and bones of dead cattle scattered around these ponds.

Jesse came riding up on Princess, Captain Jamison's mare.

"I need a drink of water. I have just about run myself out trying to keep the cattle out of these alkali ponds. Fill this canteen Libby. I need to take a drink to poor ole Charlie Martin. He has just about run his legs off trying to keep the animals off the alkali."

"I will Jesse, but I don't know why you even speak to that bad boy," Libby said.

She reached for the canteen and went to the water barrel and began to fill it as she followed along beside the wagon trying to not spill a drop of precious water.

"Here Jesse. I hope Charlie appreciates it more than I think he will," Libby said as she handed the canteen up to Jesse. Princess' sweat soaked coat was covered in dust.

Jesse reached for the canteen, took a long drink then tied it behind his saddle. He pulled off his hat and wiped his sweat covered face with his sleeve. "See you tonight at Independence Rock. I may not get back for the nooning. Too busy," Jesse called back over his shoulder as he rode away toward the back of the wagon train.

***

"Where is Jesse?" Papa asked at the nooning.

"He is working the cattle," Nancy answered. There is so much alkali that it is taking all the available riders to keep them moving away from it."

"They will be a tired bunch tonight," Papa said as he sat

down for the nooning meal.

"Nancy, will we be able to go to Independence Rock?" Libby asked.

"Mason is planning to go. Don't worry. He and Jesse will wash themselves up, eat supper and be able to ride over there. Mason will bring Ladyfair for me to ride and you can ride behind me," Nancy said.

"Those boys are full of vinegar and have some to spare," Papa said.

"I hope that means Charlie Martin doesn't think he can follow along," Libby said.

"Charlie Martin isn't our worry, Libby. It's Liza. She is going over with her folks and I am afraid she will get an idea that may cause trouble for herself and maybe for you, " said Mama.

"Oh, I won't listen to her Mama. I will tell her to stay safe. I think she will do what her Pa tells her to do," Libby answered.

"Let's hope she listens," Mama said

After the nooning Libby watched for the giant mound that would be Independence Rock. Liza came to walk with her. They were excited about reaching the big rock.

“It’s supposed to look like a giant turtle,” Liza said.

“I know,” answered Libby. “I hope I can find a place to write my name. There are hundreds of names on the rock they say.”

“I will find a place for my name. Papa says we can take some tar and a brush to paint our names,” Liza said.

The girls walked along beside the Campbell wagon until the middle of the afternoon when they began to see the giant form of Independence Rock

Liza turned toward Libby. “Time to get home.” she said. She waved as she hurried toward her wagon. “See you at Independence Rock.”

The wagons pulled into a circle beside the Sweetwater River and across from Independence Rock. They would camp here for the night. There was fresh, clean water from the river to wash away the dust and grime.

When supper was finished Nancy and Libby quickly cleaned up the dishes and packed things away.

“Are you and Papa going over to see the rock?” Nancy asked Mama.

“No, we will stay with Ben. Papa needs the rest,” Mama

answered.

"I will listen to everything that Nancy tells me, Mama," said Libby.

"Be sure you do that, Libby," answered Mama.

Nancy and Libby went inside the wagon to get ready. Libby washed away the dust and dirt and dressed in clean clothes. She sat down on her bed and watched as Nancy brushed her long dark hair and tied it back with a red ribbon. She wore her brown riding skirt and her white embroidered blouse. She pinched her cheeks to bring up the color and then stood and brushed down her skirt.

"Do I look all right Libby?" she asked.

"You look awfully pretty, Nancy," Libby answered. They heard the sound of horses outside the wagon and Nancy looked out the pucker hole.

"It's Mason," she said. "Lets go."

Libby watched as Nancy looked up at Mason Connors on his black horse, Paladin, and smiled. Mason handed the reins of another horse, a mare named Ladyfair, to her.

"She is gentle and Libby will be safe riding behind you," Mason said.

Papa gave Nancy a boost up and then helped Libby on behind Nancy.

"Hold tight and stay right with your sister, Libby," Papa said.

"I will Papa," Libby answered.

They rode the short distance to the giant rock where Mason tied the horses. The rock was lower on one end and they decided to look at the names written there. There were hundreds of names written by earlier immigrants. Mason found the name of one of his former neighbors.

"This is the name of our neighbor dated two years ago. It was written on his way to Oregon. We heard from him once and he says Oregon is a great country. I brought some tar to write our names."

Libby scrambled up the giant rock behind Mason and Nancy. It was hard to keep from slipping on the hard surface. She pulled herself up over a rough spot by grabbing a little bush that grew in a crevice.

Nancy turned back to look at Libby. "Are you doing all right, Libby?" she asked.

"I'm coming. I am coming just fine," she said as she puffed out her breath."

"Sounds like you need a rest," Mason said. "Right up there is a flat place and I think there may be room for our names. Let's move on up and see."

Mason brushed away the dirt and found a small place that had no names. He wrote his name first, then Nancy's. Just as Libby started her name she heard a shout from below.

"Libby. Libby Campbell. I can see you up there."

It was Liza and her Ma and Pa. They began climbing up the rock.

"We are coming up." Liza shouted.

Libby hurried and finished her name. They all stood back and looked at their work.

"I think it needs a date," said Mason.

"Write July 12, 1847," said Nancy.

Mason finished the date and they stood waiting for Liza and her family. Nancy whispered into Libby's ear.

"Stay with me. Don't run away with Liza."

"That is nice writing," Liza said when she reached them. "We want to write our names too."

"Looks like we better look for another place since that one is full," Mr. Stampers said.

Mr. and Mrs. Stampers walked up further but Liza stayed behind.

"I'll bet I can find a spot for our names. Want to come with me Libby?"

"No, I will stay with Nancy and Mason."

"Oh, come on scaredy cat. We can climb up to that bush up there above us. That isn't far."

Libby took a step forward then stopped. She wanted to see what was up higher. It would be fun to explore with Liza. She took another step forward and then another behind Liza as she scrambled up.

"Come on, slow poke. Let's get going," Liza called. d

"Libby stopped. She could hear Mama's voice telling her, "Stay with Nancy."

She looked back at Nancy who had put her fingers on her hips and stood with feet apart shaking her head no.

Libby looked back toward Liza. "Can't go," she said.

"Can't go? You'll miss all the fun."

"Sorry, Liza. I need to stay with Nancy and Mason."

See you later then, " called Liza as she hurried up toward the bush.

"There are some names of famous men written here on this rock," Mason said. "Colonel John C. Fremont, the famous explorer of the west, carved his name here. I think it is higher up on the rock."

"Let's climb a bit higher and look out at the view," Nancy said.

"Are you up to climbing higher, Libby?" Mason asked.

"Sure, I can go higher," Libby answered.

They climbed up slowly, stopping to rest after reaching a level place on the rock. Libby looked up ahead to see if she could see Liza but all she could see was bare rock. She felt the wind against her face. She stood still listening to it roar in her ears and the pop of her skirt as it whipped against her legs.

A sharp scream came from up on the rock. It was loud at first and then grew faint.

Mason said, "Let's go. That could be Liza needing help."

They scrambled up the rock toward the bush where Liza had been going. Mason and Nancy hurried and Libby struggled to keep up. Mason soon reached the little bush and Nancy was right behind him. Libby slipped and scooted and fell down on her knees then pushed her hands against the rock and got up again to climb higher.

When she reached Mason and Nancy, Mason was lying on his stomach listening to the sounds coming from a deep crevice in the rock. "I can hear someone down there. This hole is big enough for Liza to have slipped through. Find Mr. and Mrs. Stampers and I'll go down and get a rope from my saddle."

"Oh, Nancy, could Liza be hurt?" Libby asked.

"Let's hope not. Come help me find Mr and Mrs. Stampers."

"I think they went over there," Libby said as she pointed across the big rock.

"I think I see them. Isn't that Mrs. Stampers sun bonnet?" Nancy asked.

"Libby put her hands up and cupped her mouth calling, " Mr. Stampers, Mrs. Stampers. Come here," she called as she ran behind Nancy.

Mrs Stampers shaded her eyes putting her hand on the brim of her sun bonnet and stood watching the girls as they ran.

"Mrs Stampers, Nancy panted as she reached them. Come

quickly. We think Liza may have fallen in a crevice."

"Isn't she with you girls? I thought she stayed behind with you."

"No, Ma'am," Libby insisted.

Mr. Stampers jumped forward and started running up the rock.

Mrs. Stampers reached out and gripped Nancy's arm. "Oh please, Nancy, pray that it isn't Liza."

"Let's hurry back to that bush. That's where Mason found the hole. He has gone to get a rope."

When they reached the bush Mason had a rope that he dangled into the hole. Mr. Stampers lay on his stomach calling.

"Liza, is that you down there?"

There was no answer.

"Liza, listen to me. Can you see the rope? Grab it and put the loop around your waist. Get it now."

A faint answer came up from the hole below. "Papa."

"Liza, look for the rope. It is moving up and down. Grab it now," Mr Stampers called again.

I found it Papa,"

“Put it around your waist.”

There was quiet from below. Mrs. Stampers moved closer.

“Do as Pa says , Liza.”

“Can’t.” came a cry from below.

“Liza, put that rope over your head and around your waist right now,” Mr. Stampers shouted.

It was quiet with no sound from the hole. Libby brushed tears from her cheeks. Her friend might be hurt and unable to get the rope. Mrs. Stampers started to cry too.

“Ma, no time for crying. Get closer and call down to her.”

“Liza, get the rope over your head and pull it around you. You can do it Liza? Remember you are as tough as a pine knot.

I’m tough Ma,” Liza called faintly.

They waited listening for sounds from below. Mason held the rope steady and felt a slight tug on it.

“I got it Pa,” Liza called.

“Is the rope on Liza,” Mr. Stampers called.

“I have it around my waist, Pa.”

“Good girl, Liza. Now hold on to the rope above your head with both hands and use your feet to push away from the wall,”

Mr Stampers called.

Very slowly Mason pulled the rope against the rock at the edge of the hole. Mr. Stampers pulled behind Mason and Nancy and Mrs. Stampers pulled behind him. At the end of the rope Libby held on as tight as she could.

"Keep coming Liza," called Mr Stampers.

"I will Pa," Liza called.

At last Liza's head appeared. She gripped the edge of the hole with both hands and pulled but could not get through the narrow hole. A rock cap lay over a part of the opening.

"Let's tie the rope off around this bush. Both of us can then help her around that cap," said Mason

After pushing and pulling and holding tight to the rope Liza was at last out of the hole. She lay on her back looking up at the sky then reached for her Ma's outstretched arms and buried her face against her mother.

"Liza, we need to check you out. to see if you are hurt," Mr. Stampers said.

I think my arm is broken Pa. It hurts like a fiery furnace," Liza said.

“Yep, that arm is is broken all right, I am sorry to say.”

“We can use my petticoat to make a sling until we get home,” said Nancy. She stepped in front of Mrs. Stampers and slipped out of her white petticoat.

A sling was made for Liza’s arm and Mr Stampers carried Liza down the rock. Mason, Mrs. Stampers, Nancy and Libby followed behind.

They reached the bottom of the rock, mounted their horses and rode back to the camp.

At the Stampers wagon Mason asked, ”Should I ride back to the train behind us and ask for the doctor? There is supposed to be one in that train.”

“I’m much obliged Mason but you have already done more than I could expect. I’ll help get Liza cleaned up and put to bed and then I will ride for the doctor.”

When Liza was helped from Mr. Stampers horse, Libby put her arm around her friend and whispered, “Don’t worry, Liza. You will be fine. I just know it.”

“I will,” answered Liza and she sniffed at the tears that started to fall.

DEVIL'S GATE

As soon as she awoke the next morning Libby asked for permission to go see Liza. When Mama said yes, she hurried to the Stamper wagon. The doctor had come and set Liza's arm. Now she sat on her bed in the wagon with her forehead scrunched up in a wrinkly frown.

"Does it hurt, Liza?" asked Libby.

"No, it doesn't hurt much but what can I do with a arm that won't work and is stiff as a board with this apparatus they put it in? I can't do much now but sit."

"You can still walk can't you?"

"I can walk but not very far. Ma and Pa said I had to stay within sight of our wagon unless they gave their permission for me to go anywhere else. You see I am being punished for running off on Independence Rock. When I fell in the hole it gave them a scare so now I'm stuck here."

"I will walk with you Liza beside your wagon. We will go past Devil's Gate today. It's where the Sweetwater river cuts through the tall rock cliffs. It will be fun to see it."

"Well, I suppose so but I would have liked it better before I hurt my arm. Now, I can't do anything but walk."

"After breakfast I'll be back and we can walk together," Libby said and hurried away toward the Campbell wagon.

***

Before the wagons reached Devil's Gate, the sound of rushing water could be heard. The oxen plodded along the Sweetwater River. The grass was green and beautiful wildflowers sprinkled it with a rainbow of colors.

"Did you ever see so many wildflowers?, asked Libby.

"Don't guess so," mumbled Liza.

"Hey, are you still in a grumpy mood Liza?," asked Libby.

"Well, I don't mean to be, but this arm is a pain and wearing this old sling around my neck scratches me. I guess I am just going to be grumpy until I can take it off," Liza said.

"Let's hurry over there to where the people are standing and see if we can see the water going through the gate."

The stone walls rose high up on each side of a narrow cut made by the river as it splashed and surged through the small opening made after many years of washing through the wall. The sound of rushing water filled the air and tiny droplets of water rose up catching the sunlight and were turned into sparkling crystal.

The girls walked as close as they dared, catching the spray from the water that dampened their faces and hair. Liza laughed and wiped her face with her hand.

"Yikes," she said. "A body could get wet here if they aren't careful."

"It's fun though isn't it Liza?" Libby asked. "Let's pick some wildflowers and carry them back to the wagons."

"I can pick some with my good hand and pile them in my apron pocket I guess. Mama will like them."

The girls gathered blue, yellow, red, and pink flowers until Liza's apron pocket was stretched out full of flowers. Libby carried her apron folded over the sprays of flowers that she had picked. They started back toward the wagons.

"Oh, look, Liza. There are two new graves over there. They walked over the grass along the river to a rock ledge. At the bottom of the ledge were two graves with markers made from boards.

"We have seen lots of graves along the way," said Liza. But you can tell these were made not long ago. The dirt is still fresh and the writing on the markers is still plain enough."

"One grave is small," said Libby. "Wonder who it belongs to?"

"Go ahead and read the name why don't you?"

"Albert John Martin, July 2, 1845, Died July 6, 18, 1847. He was only two years old when he died," said Libby. Maybe that is his Mama's grave next to his. Elizabeth May Martin is her name. I wonder what happened. Did they get sick or get hurt?"

The girls sat down on the ground beside the small grave and looked at the little mound.

"I think it is a sad story, what ever happened," Liza said. " I think we should put some of the flowers we gathered on the graves. I am going to leave some yellow daisies on Elizabeth's grave," she said and placed the beautiful yellow blooms at the head of the grave.

"I'll put some blue phlox on baby Albert's grave. He must have been a merry boy, laughing as he took his first wobbly steps," said Libby. "My brother Ben was like that when he was trying to walk."

The girls sat together in silence near the graves. They could hear the rush of the Sweetwater River in the distance and the lonely sound of the wind blowing through the sage brush. They brushed away tears that were determined to creep down their cheeks as they thought about the mother and her baby boy lying silently in their graves, their family long gone, far across the mountains.

Libby stretched her arm across Liza's shoulders and Liza leaned her head against her friend.

"It is so sad Libby," said Liza.

"Yes, it is," Libby answered. "There are too many graves along the trail."

Liza stood up and brushed off her skirt. "Let's make our Mas happy by bringing them some flowers."

"Yes, before they wilt in the sun," Libby agreed and the girls walked away from the graves not looking back as they started toward the wagons.

SOUTH PASS

The Campbell family stood by their wagons looking out to the west at the wide smooth valley of South Pass.

"We have reached the Continental Divide," said Papa. "We are now half way to the Columbia River and the Willamette Valley. From now on all waters will run west. We can say good-bye to the East and all that we knew there."

"We have come a long way but you say we are only half way there?" Jesse asked.

"Half way is right and from now on it will be over rough rocks and steep mountains. We may have to lighten our load to help out the oxen. They are pretty worn down now."

"I hope we can keep our cooking utensils," Mama said.

"They are some of the last things we will give up," Papa answered. "So far, our mules and oxen have been strong but we have rough traveling ahead of us."

"Half way, half way. We are only half way to Oregon," rang in Libby's ears. Her feet suddenly felt very heavy as she dragged them across the dirt beside the wagon. She reached Mama's side and Mama put her arm around Libby's waist.

"Don't think of it as so many long, weary days ahead but think of just one more day to travel," Mama said.

"But Mama, there are so many days ahead and I am so tired. I am so tired of the dust and tired of the flies and tired of bacon and beans."

"I know, Libby, It isn't like home but we will see so many beautiful sights and you have Liza as a friend. What about that Libby? Won't you two have fun?"

All Libby could do was climb inside the wagon and sob. She lay on her bed and cried tears of frustration. Finally, when she was too tired to cry, she jumped up, wiped her face, brushed her hair, and stepped outside the wagon. The sun was just at the top of the distant mountain tops. It would be night soon.

"Feeling better now?" Mama asked and gave Libby a hug.

"I'm sorry, Mama. Sometimes I just get so tired."

"I know Libby," she answered. "We all get tired and weary of the things we have to do on this long trail. We will reach its end and we will find a good home in Oregon. I'll tell you a secret. I have had myself a good cry too now and then."

"You did, Mama? I didn't know you felt bad enough to cry. I didn't think Mamas were supposed to cry.

After you cried did feel better?

"I did and I got back to work and made myself useful again. It isn't easy for any of us but we are strong people and we will get to Oregon."

"I can make myself useful too, Mama. I will help with supper. I want to help us get to Oregon

"Good Libby. You can stir the stew for me while I mix the bread."

"And this time I won't catch my skirt on fire." Libby answered.

***

After supper, Libby and Nancy went to the wagon to work on the leather jacket for Jesse. Nancy stitched the seams and Libby worked cutting fringe.

"I think the jacket is starting to look nice Nancy," said Libby.

"Yes, it is starting to take shape. We need to put the fringe on the sleeves before I sew them up. do you have enough ready, Libby?"

"There should be more than enough. See this long strip and here is another one I've finished."

" That's probably enough for two sleeves. I'll sew it on next and then we can sew up the sleeves," Nancy said.

The girls worked under the lantern light until they could no longer hear voices outside. The shadows inside the wagon were dim now and the light from the campfires was almost gone.

"We had best put this away and get to bed or we will both be sleepyheads in the morning."

"You're right, Libby. I was so busy with my sewing I forgot about the time. Let's put this into the old pillow case and I will hide it under my bed. So far, I don't think Jesse suspects anything,"

"I don't think so either and he still won't mention his missing mare. I think he believes we have all forgotten about it. How could we ever forget? I know I won't forget, not ever, " Libby said.

"I won't forget it either but maybe the jacket will help Jesse know we all feel sad about Maggie and want to help make him be happy again," Nancy answered.

"Here is the fringe I made. I think it looks nice."

"It looks perfect Libby. Now under the bed it goes until we can work on it again."

***

“Everybody out of the wagons,” called Captain Jamison.

Libby watched as the oxen stretched their big heads forward and strained against their yokes as they climbed the steep grade up the mountain. Papa and Jesse tied a rope to the wagon and then wound it around a tree to make sure the wagon didn’t roll backward. As the oxen slowly moved forward they let the rope slide around the tree to release the tension and allow the oxen to move on.

“Ho!” called Captain Jamison. “Stop your wagons. These animals need a rest.”

Chains rattled, cattle bawled and dust flew up in clouds, then the wagon train was still.

The captain spoke in a firm voice, “Now folks, we have to lighten the load to help get these wagons over this mountain. Get rid of anything except what is going to help keep you alive. ”

Libby hurried to catch up with Mama who started running toward the wagon when she saw Papa and Jesse climbing into the back.

“Wait now Papa, Mama called. Let me help you choose what’s to go.”

Out came Mama’s writing desk, the fireplace tools, the

wooden breadbox, Papa's shoe mending last and then with Jesse pushing and Papa lifting, out came Grandma's oak dresser.

"Oh my," Mama said. "I dearly do hate to leave the dresser. It was made by my grandfather and It has been in our family for so many years. "

Mama turned away and covered her face with her apron. Libby ran to her and squeezed her hand and Nancy came and put her arms around Mama's shoulders as she sobbed.

"It's alright Mama. We will get you another dresser. When we get to Oregon we will find someone who can make one for you," Nancy spoke softly.

They stood together while Papa and Jesse rolled the dresser away from the trail until it tumbled down the mountain. They heard it crash on some rocks below.

"No-oo-oo. A wail sounded above the clatter and noise of the wagons.

"Whatever has happened?" Mama asked and looked up the mountain side. Libby and Nancy ran to the front of the wagon.

A rush of gravel and dust came sliding down behind Liza as she came running down the mountain to the Campbell's wagons.

"Oh, Libby, Ma is so sad. She is screaming so loud because Pa had to throw away our butter churn and stove. She says she can never feed the family without em. What can I do? Ma just can't stop crying and Pa says he can't help it because our oxen are weak. Briny has sore hoofs and Betsy is plum wore out and he has to lighten the load."

Libby put her arms around Liza and hugged her. "I know Liza. Mama had to give up her oak dresser that had been in the family a long time. It's so sad. Go put your arms around your Mama and let her know you love her. Love's the best thing anyway, better than some old furniture."

"All right, Libby. I'll go find Ma and tell her I will help her with a camp fire for the cooking. As long as we're together we'll get by."

With a flurry of dust Liza raced up the mountain toward her family's wagon.

"Let's load up now, Papa called. We need to be ready when the wagons move on."

Libby, Nancy, and Mama put their heads inside the back of the wagon. It was a different place with lots of room down the middle and one big empty space where the dresser had been. Mama turned around and gave her apron a jerk and said,

"Well, so be it. That's what it's come to, so we might as well get going."

The wheels rose up on top of big rocks and then crashed down to the ground making the wagon bounce, and Little Ben had to hold tight to the seat to keep from falling. Papa urged the mules ahead and they strained to pull the heavy load. Men shouted and the crack of bull whips filled the air. The wagons slowly inched their way up.

***

"Let's get the fire started," Mama said. "We are all so tired after such a struggle up through the dust and steep climb."

"I'll go help Will and Jesse water the oxen and wash the dust off their faces."

"All right Libby. After that, come back and help with supper," Mama said.

Libby took a water bucket and went to the water barrel and filled it and with water and with an old rag washed the dusty faces of the the oxen. Their big heads were covered with dust. Their lashes were so full of it that when they blinked their eyes, dust fell from their lashes into their eyes. Libby carefully wiped away the dust and the animals shook their dusty coats.

Supper was finished and dishes put away and the tired travelers were soon in bed. Libby listened to the strange sounds. There were the sounds of animals rustling through the loose sticks and leaves. A coyote called yip, yip, yip and the lonely cry of a wolf came from high up on a mountain. Libby scooted down deep into the covers on her bed. The wolf's call always made her shiver. She pulled her covers up to her chin and lay very still. Before she heard the wolf again she was asleep.

***

After a cold night the morning sun was heartily welcomed. Mama filled a skillet with corn cakes, flipping them over at just the right time. The fire underneath popped and cracked as flames reached up to touch the bottom of the iron spider and the smell of pine smoke filled the air. The family gathered around the cook fire and got their share of corn cakes and molasses and bacon.

"It will be another hard day for the teams," Jesse said.

"We haven't even got to the steep part yet," Papa said. Let's get the teams harnessed and be ready to go when the call comes to move out," Papa said.

Libby helped Mama and Nancy pack the cooking things in the wagon. They shook out the bedding and packed the tent.

They were ready when Captain Jamison called, "Move out."

Libby walked beside the wagon. When she had to walk over rough rocks and fallen limbs she got behind. Mama came back to look for her.

"Libby," Mama scolded, "you need to keep up with us. It is dangerous for you to walk alone. We're told there could be hostile Indians on this trail."

"But Mama, my feet are sore and these rocks hurt so bad."

"Well, get out your shoes and put them on."

"The soles are half worn out. They have big holes right in the middle."

"Go ahead and wear them. They will help some. When Papa rests the team get inside the wagon and put them on."

When Papa stopped the wagon, Libby climbed in and found her high topped leather shoes. She held them up then turned them over to look at the big round holes in the middle of each sole.

"The rocks can come right through," she said in disgust. "Might as well try to put in something to cover up the holes. Maybe some scraps of leather we had left over from Jesse's jacket."

She quickly pulled out the bag holding the unfinished jacket from under Nancy's bed. She laid the bag aside and and found two scraps big enough to cover the holes. She stuffed these inside her shoes, then put them on and laced quickly them up.

"Ho! Get up there Prince," Papa called.

The wagon lurched forward. Libby grabbed hold of the end of her bed but the boards under it moved forward and fell down to the floor of the wagon. She quickly put them back in place and was straightening her covers when Mama called.

"Libby get out of the wagon. The mules are pulling too hard and we need to lighten the load."

"I'm coming Mama."

A short time later the team stopped again and Papa and Jesse came to the back of the wagon. Libby saw them and ran ahead. She quickly looked on Nancy's bed for the bag with Jesse's jacket to hide it. She looked up and down the bed and then moved the covers aside and looked some more. When she didn't see it, she got down on her knees and looked under the bed. There was no bag there. It was gone. Jesse's jacket was gone.

"Oh, No-ooo!" she wailed. The jacket must have fallen out

the back when the wagon lurched. "What can I do?" she sobbed.

"What's the matter Libby?" Papa called from just outside the wagon's pucker hole.

"I'm alright Papa. My feet have been getting sore through these holes in my shoes," she said.

"I promise I'll try to fix those shoes tonight, Libby."

"All right, Papa," Libby answered.

Libby ran back down the trail to try and find the jacket. It might be lying on the ground somewhere. She searched along the wagon tracks and under bushes that were beside the trail. She got farther and farther away from their wagon until she had come to the last wagon of their train.

"Are you one of the Campbell children?" the woman in the wagon asked.

"Yes, I am," answered Libby.

"Well, child, you better get back to your wagon. Don't walk back any more. We are the last wagon and it is dangerous for you to go back by yourself."

"Yes, Ma'am," answered Libby and ran back up the trail

looking under wagons and bushes as she ran.

As much as she looked, there was no old pillowcase with a leather jacket inside.

She heard Mama calling, "Libby, Libby come home now. It's going to be dark soon. Catch up to the wagon right away."

She ran over rocks and around bushes. She felt a sharp rock against the bottom of her foot and looked down at the sole of her shoe. There was no leather there. It had fallen out of her shoe. When she checked the other foot that leather was gone too.

"All for nothing. I lost Jesse's jacket all for nothing."

Her head drooped when she realized that the jacket was gone for good. How could she tell Nancy and Mama? How disappointed Mama would be. *Maybe I don't have to tell them right away,* she thought.

Supper was cooked and the family sat near the cook fire. Jesse threw on some more wood and the flames leaped up under the trees. The smell of smoke and cooked bacon filled the air. Libby sat beside the fire not saying anything. She bent her chin down thinking about the missing jacket.

"What's the matter Libby? Isn't your old chatterbox working?" asked Jesse. "It seems like you are mighty quiet tonight."

"Yes, Libby, are you feeling poorly tonight?" Mama asked.

"Well, I did promise Libby to fix her worn out shoes," said Papa. Let's get on with it my girl. We will give your poor, sore feet a rest."

Papa took the awl, a big needle, and a piece of buffalo hide out of the tool box. Libby took off her shoes and laid them beside Papa. He cut a thin strip from the the buffalo hide. He then cut two pieces of buffalo hide just the size to fit inside the shoes and carefully sewed the leather piece to the shoe sole. When they were finished Libby put them on and jumped up and down.

"At last, Papa, my feet feel good."

"Yes, Libby. Maybe they will last a while."

Libby ran back and forth testing her shoes.

"If you have that much energy, Libby, we should go to the wagon and work on our sewing," Nancy said.

Libby didn't answer. She turned her head and looked away from Nancy.

"Come on Libby. Let's get going," Nancy said.

Libby dragged her feet as she followed Nancy back to the

wagon. When they climbed inside, Libby sat down on her bed and Nancy bent down and looked under her bed. She looked up suddenly and stared at Libby.

"The bag is gone. Libby, our bag that had the jacket inside is gone!"

Libby's face puckered up and she bowed her head and covered her eyes with her hands. Her thin shoulders shook from her sobs.

"Libby, whatever has happened? What is wrong?"

"Oh, Nancy," Libby cried. "It's all my fault. I lost the jacket. The whole bag fell out of the wagon when we were going up the mountain. The wagon gave a big jerk and I just know it fell out then."

"But how could it fall out of the wagon? It was stuffed tight under my bed?"

Libby sobbed louder until her sobs turned into a loud wail and echoed from the wagon. Mama came running and climbed inside the wagon.

"Girls what's wrong? What ever is the matter, Libby? Are you hurt?"

Libby reached out and wound her arms around Mama's

waist. "Oh Mama, I wanted some leather scraps to put inside my shoes to fill up the holes and I got the bag out and before I could put it back under the bed, the wagon gave a big lurch and it must have fallen out. Now it's gone. I went to look for it, all the way back to the end of the train, but I couldn't find it. It's gone for good. I am so sorry, Mama. What can I do? Jesse won't have a jacket to surprise him."

No one spoke and only Libby's deep sobs were heard inside the wagon. Their faces were sad and tears ran down their cheeks. Libby started to wail again as she clung to Mama.

Mama stroked Libby's hair and said, "Stop, Libby. Stop crying. There is nothing to be done but try to figure out a different way to surprise Jesse. We are all disappointed that the jacket is gone and chances are we will never see it again. Now let's get to bed and let this rest for the night."

Nancy stood up and reached her arms around Mama and Libby. They leaned their heads together and cried. Libby squeezed Nancy's hand, hoping that she would forgive her.

"I'm sorry that it happened Libby," Nancy said. "I wish it wasn't so and I know you didn't mean to, but it hurts so much that all our work is gone and there is nothing left for Jesse."

"Yes, Libby," Mama said. This is so hurtful and not something we will easily forget. You must always take care and think ahead. We will try to think of something else to surprise Jesse. Goodnight girls."

The two girls got ready for bed in silence. That night, Libby lay in her bed thinking about Jesse and what could be a good surprise for him. As hard as she thought nothing seemed right. She grew tired of thinking and turned away from her sister's bed to stare at the white wagon cover, then she fell asleep.

THE WILD MARE

The wagons moved out early next morning. The trail was rough and to avoid a bumpy ride, the family walked beside the wagon except for Little Ben, who held tight to the seat as the mules pulled up the steep trail.

Libby was quiet as she walked. She could think of nothing else but how she had lost Jesse's jacket. Her head jerked up suddenly when she heard someone shout.

"Jesse! Hey, Jesse! Where is Jesse?" called Charlie Martin as he came running up to the Campbell wagon.

"Where do you think he is?" shouted Libby. "He is where you should be, back herding the cattle. Isn't that supposed to be your job?"

"But I got to see him right away," Charlie said as he turned and ran toward the back of the wagon train.

"Now what do you think that bad boy wants with Jesse?" Libby asked.

"Who knows?" Nancy answered. "I hope he is not up to something he shouldn't be. Jesse doesn't need anymore trouble from him."

"It can't be easy for that boy to walk back there with all the dust trying to help herd the animals. Jesse says he is working hard, trying to do what is right," Mama replied.

"I wonder how Jesse can look at him let alone work with him after what he did. Jesse would still have his mare if it hadn't been for Charlie," Nancy said.

"I hope I never have to lay my eyes on him again," said Libby.

"We will probably see him again as long as his family is in the train," Mama answered.

It was near time for the wagons to stop for nooning when Jesse came riding fast.

"Papa," he called. Charlie Martin says there's a wild mare with a new born foal in a gully just back of the train. I would like to try to catch her and tame her. Could you help me Papa?" Jesse shouted, excitement in his voice and dark hair flying around his red face as he rode Princess up to the wagon.

Papa drove the mules over to the side of the trail and Will brought the freight wagon up behind.

"That mare probably left the herd to foal in a quiet place. She wouldn't be easy to catch. She would be wild and and hard to tame. The foal might not be able to keep up with the train. We would need some help to have any hope of catching her," Papa said.

"Charlie said his Pa would help us. Look, they have pulled off the trail up ahead. Please Papa, give me a chance to get another horse. I can tame her. And I won't forget about my herding chores," Jesse pleaded.

"Seems to me you want to take on more than you can handle my boy," Papa answered and stood with his hands on his hips looking up at Jesse.

Jesse's red face scrunched up into a frown and his lips stretched tight as he tried to hold in his anger.

Papa watched Jesse, as he sat on Princess, not saying a word.

Finally, he said, "Well, if you're determined, then get some rope out of the wagon. We'll need all we have for this chore,"

Libby watched as Charlie Martin and his father came running to join Papa and Jesse. "May I come watch?" she asked in a high pitched voice.

Papa turned toward Libby and in a firm, voice said, "No. You need to stay with the wagon and help your Mama take care of the mules and oxen. They need water."

Libby replied in a soft voice, "I will Papa."

Libby helped Mama and Nancy carry buckets of water from the water barrel to give the mules and oxen a drink. When the chores were finished, she stood looking into the distance listening for any sound of horses or men but she could hear only the sigh of the wind. Feeling left out and lonely, she looked in the wagon for her school reader and sat down under the shade of the wagon cover. Clouds covered the hot sun in the late afternoon and a cool breeze swept across her face. Libby fell asleep.

***

Eee-eee!

Libby jumped up when she heard a horse's whinny. She ran to the back of the wagon to get a better look.

She could see horses coming toward her. Princess was in front and Charlie Martin was in the saddle. Behind on one side was Jesse and Papa and on the other side was Mr. Martin and Will. They had ropes on a spotted mare. Each time the spotted mare tried to rear up, scream and paw the air, she was quickly pulled down with the ropes. Behind the mare walked a wobbly little foal, bay in color, with a white blaze across its face.

Libby jumped up and down and clapped her hands. "They did it! They did it!" she shouted. "They got the mare and her colt." She brushed her hands across her face to get her hair away from her eyes, so that she could get a better look. Not being able to see much better she suddenly dashed ahead toward the oncoming horses.

"Get back, Libby! Get back," shouted Jesse. "Go back to the wagon."

Libby stopped and turned around in frustration. As much as she wanted to be a part of things she just couldn't. She stood behind the freight wagon and waited. Mama and Nancy went to the mules and tried to quiet them as they pawed the ground and strained in their harness from the excitement of the coming horses.

"Out of the way Libby," called Papa. Libby ran to the front wagon and stood watching as the men tied the spotted mare to the freight wagon tightening the ropes until she could barely move. The little colt nuzzled up under his mother to get a drink of warm milk.

Jesse talked to the mare in a soft, crooning voice. "Whoa now. Whoa girl. There now girl. We won't hurt you."

"Best to leave her alone for awhile now," Papa said. She's

about wore herself out and needs to settle down away from us for awhile."

Charlie Martin looked toward Libby but she turned her back and refused to look at him. He shrugged his shoulder and turned and walked with his Pa toward his family's wagon.

Papa checked the mules and said, " Let's be on our way and maybe we can catch up with the train by evening. Jesse and Will are going to stay with the mare until she settles down."

"I want to help Papa," I want to help Jesse with the wild mare and her baby," Libby begged in a soft, insistent voice.

"The mare needs to get used to Jesse first. She is a wild animal and can strike out with those hoofs and be dangerous. I expect she can bite too. She has a baby to protect and will keep her baby safe in any way that she can. Jesse will slowly get acquainted with her and eventually she should trust him. You can help out then Libby."

***

The sun, a giant red ball, was just at the edge of the horizon when the Campbell wagon reached the wagon train. They hurried to enter the circle of wagons and set up their tent and start their cooking fire. By the time the sun slid down out of sight they were ready to sit down around the campfire for supper.

"Wonder what Jesse and Will are having for supper," Nancy said.

"If I know Will and his cooking, it will be bacon and beans," said Papa.

"I don't think that is as good as our dried buffalo stew," added Libby.

Mama said, "I know for sure they won't go hungry. Will has done his share of trail cooking and he will make a good supper."

The family sat around the fire until there were just a few red coals in the fire pit. They listened for sounds of the wild mare and her colt, but when there was no sound of them, only the yip, yip of coyotes.

***

The wagons moved out in the early morning. There was still no sign of Jesse, Will, or the mare and her colt. Libby followed along behind the family wagon. She saw Liza waiting for her up ahead and hurried to meet her.

"Liza," she called. "Know what happened last night?" she

asked in an excited voice.

"Guess I don't," answered Liza.

"We had some real excitement last night. Jesse caught a wild mare and her colt and they are back on the trail until he can tame her a little."

"Jesse caught a wild mare all by himself? Hump, that seems like a powerful story to me. Nobody could catch a wild mare by themselves. Nobody I know could do that. Not even Jesse."

"Well, he had some help. Will and Papa and Mr. Martin and that mean boy of his helped get her."

"Tell me truly. Did that ornery Charlie Martin get close enough to Jesse to help him do something? I would think Jesse wouldn't want him to come any closer than he would want to get to a pole cat."

"Jesse couldn't do it by himself and Charlie Martin was the one who found the mare so I guess Jesse let him help because he wanted the mare so much."

"Things sure do change don't they?"

"I still don't like Charlie Martin. No, not one bit do I like him. I don't forget about Jesse's mare, Maggie, and I don't forget about that old rattlesnake either."

"I reckon not. It would take powerful forgetin to forget that. I'm glad Jesse got himself a mare though. I can't wait to see her."

"Yes, and she has a foal too."

"Is it a boy or a girl? Do you know?"

"Not yet I don't, but I am thinking it's a colt. You know, a boy."

"I hope they catch up soon don't you Libby?"

"They'll be here as soon as they can. Papa don't want them to be back so far by themselves."

"Maybe they will catch up by the time we get to Ft. Bridger."

"We might not make it there until tomorrow Papa says," Libby answered.

"Woops! We've got to catch up with our wagons. Look, they are way ahead," Liza warned.

The girls ran to catch up and were hot and dusty when they reached the Campbell wagon.

***

"See the mountains up there Libby? They look close but Pa

says they are far, far away. I could use a big bite of that white snow I see up there couldn't you Libby?"

"It would taste awfully good, Liza. It would taste awfully good. Mama says when we find some snow we can make snow ice cream. You just mix some milk and eggs and sugar and put the snow in it and just like magic ,you've got ice cream."

"If you still have sugar and eggs you sure are lucky cause ours has been used up."

Ma says it will probably be too costly at Ft. Bridger but I sure would like to make some snow ice cream."

"Me too, Lizzie."

"I'll see you later, Libby," Liza said and ran ahead to her family wagon.

The Campbell wagon bumped up and down over the rough trail and Libby walked beside Mama and Nancy. They followed the wagons down into the valley where the Black's Fork of the Green River ran through a beautiful green valley. They could see the brown logs of the buildings of Ft. Bridger as they walked down towards it.

"What a beautiful place this is. Look at the green grass waving and the trees along the streams are so beautiful," Mama said.

“I can’t wait to get into the water,” said Libby.

She grabbed Nancy’s hand and the two girls ran ahead of the wagons and were soon outside the log walls of the fort. They stood outside the fort”s heavy log gate waiting for the wagons to arrive.There were some Indian fur traders camped outside the fort as well as a few wagons with their once white tops now tattered and dusty. From inside the fort came the sound of pounding metal against metal.

“There must be a blacksmith shop inside from all that pounding. Papa said we would be lucky to find a smithy here to help us with the wagon rims,” Nancy said.

“What’s wrong with the wagon rims?” Libby asked.

“Oh, with all the heat the wooden wheels shrink and then the metal rims are too big and they sometimes fall off,” answered Nancy. “ Papa will want to make them fit better. ”

The Campbell wagons pulled out of the train and rolled up to the fort’s gate. A tall man in buckskin clothes opened the big gate and strode over to Papa as he climbed down from the wagon.

“Bridger is my name. Jim Bridger. Welcome to our fort,” he said.

Papa reached out his hand to Mr. Bridger. " I am pleased to meet such a famous mountain man Mr. Bridger," Papa said and the two men shook hands.

"You folks can camp over there under the trees," Mr. Bridger said.

"Do you have the services of a blacksmith here Mr. Bridger? " Papa asked.

"Yes sir. You're in luck cause the smithy is working today. Times are when he's off to the mountains to hunt but you caught him here today."

We'll be needing some wheel work done." Papa said.

"Pull your wagons over there and then come on into the fort. The blacksmith shop is inside."

Captain Jamison directed the wagon train to some tall trees. Papa worked to pull off one of the big wheels from the family wagon and rolled it toward the fort gate. Little Ben ran behind Papa trying to keep up.

"Come along Ben," Papa said. "You can see how a black-smith works with a hammer and forge."

Mama, Nancy and Libby dusted off their bonnets and skirts and walked to the cool water.

“Bet I can get that dirt off your face, Nancy,” Libby said as she reached down into the water and splashed it up on to Nancy’s face.

“Oh no you don’t. You can’t get away with that, Libby, ” Nancy said as she splashed water onto Libby, wetting the front of her dress.

The girls splashed more water laughing and splashing until their dresses were dripping with water and their bonnets dangled down their backs leaving their hair open to the water sprays until it dripped in muddy tendrils around their cheeks.

Mama stood watching with her hands on her hips laughing at the girls’ fun.

“You girls make me want to jump into that water and get wet.”

“Well, why not? It’s time we got the dust off,” shouted Nancy and she jumped down into the water going under and coming up splashing and pushing her wet hair away from her face. ”Come on in you two. The water feels good.”

Libby went flying off the bank straight into the water. Bouncing up and down she called out, “Come on in Mama. It feels so good.”

Mama took off her shoes then slid feet first into the water.

They splashed each other and ducked their heads to get the last bit of dust out of their hair.

"This water feels wonderful," Mama said as she stood waist deep, twisting her long hair, wringing out the water until it no longer ran down her face. "But I expect it's time to go find some dry clothes. It will be supper time soon and Papa will be ready for it when he gets the wagon wheel fixed."

"But wasn't it fun, Mama? Wasn't it fun to get all wet and get cooled off?" asked Libby.

"It was really good fun wasn't it Mama?" Nancy asked.

"Girls, this is one of the most fun times we have had on the trail but before our neighbors over there in those wagons come out and find us dripping wet in our dresses we best get inside the wagon and find some dry clothes," Mama answered.

They found dry clothes and their wet hair was combed to hang down their backs to dry. The wet clothes were hung in the sun on bushes that grew along the stream. Nancy, Libby and Mama were in a happy mood as they started a fire for supper and got out the pot and cooking spider.

***

The family sat around the fire and ate. After supper the

dishes were put away and Papa sat quietly watching the bright red coals of the campfire. The campfires of the other campers twinkled in the evening dusk and sparks sometimes rose up into the darkness when a burned log fell down into coals to stir up the fire. There were night cries from birds and a wolf called from the mountains.

"Are you worried about Jesse, Papa?" Nancy asked.

"I am wondering what is keeping him. That wild horse could give them some trouble. Will is a good hand with horses so I don't think they will have trouble but I hope they will be here soon."

When the last coals of the camp fire died down into grey ash and the moon rose up to light up the camp, they heard a whinny. Papa ran to the end of the Fort and looked up the dark trail. In the moonlight he could see the oxen pulling Will's freight wagon and tied behind it was the wild mare with her little foal following along behind. Jesse rode Princess beside them, keeping the little fellow going along with his mother.

When they pulled up beside the gate the men from the other wagons quickly came to look the mare and her foal over.

Mr. Bridger came out and said, "Pull the wagon over there by your Pa. Good little mare you got there and she's got a foal too. She'll make you a good ridin horse."

After Jesse and Will ate supper and the flames from the supper fire were rising up to spread light around their campsite, Mr. Bridger walked into the firelight.

"I'de like to join you folks and spin a yarn," he said.

"Welcome, welcome, "Papa answered. "We would surely enjoy your company."

When they saw Mr. Bridger, some of the other campers came and sat down around the campfire. Mr. Bridger seemed to enjoy the extra company and begin to tell his story. Everyone was very quiet, the excitement of the story on their upturned faces showed in the firelight. Mr. Bridger told of being chased into a canyon by the Indians. Libby listened, waiting to see what would happen next but just as the Indians were about to reach Mr. Bridger he stopped the story and everything was quiet again. Everyone looked at Mr. Bridger, waiting for an end to the story.

The quiet remained, interrupted only by the hissing fire and the occasional sparks that flew up into the air. Mr. Bridger sat without moving, not saying a word.

When Jesse could stand the quiet no longer he jumped up

and in an excited voice shouted, "What happened next Mr. Bridger?"

Jim Bridger sat quiet for awhile longer, enjoying his rapt audience. Looking around the circle of excited faces he lifted his hands to his chest and called out in an agonized shout, "They killed me!"

The faces looked stunned for a moment. How could that be? The famous Jim Bridger killed by Indians. They looked toward the storyteller and seeing the smile on his face at the good joke he was playing on his audience, started to laugh and the hearty chuckles around the campfire grew louder as they realized the story's impossible ending. They clapped their hands and laughed some more. All the while Mr. Bridger sat still, smiling at his audience's enjoyment.

"That was a good yarn if ever I heard one, " said Papa.

"Good tale alright," another man said. "I guess it's time to turn in after that one."

The fire died down and everyone went back to their wagons. Jesse and Will checked on the mare and her foal and Mama and Papa and Little Ben went to sleep in the tent while Libby and Nancy went to sleep in the wagon.

***

Libby stirred under the warm quilts on her bed. Something had awakened her. Then she heard Liza outside the wagon.

"Wake up you sleepyhead. It is already morning and time you should be a stirin. "

Libby tumbled out of bed and reached for the pucker hole at the back of the wagon. She peeked out and saw Liza standing outside with her hands on her hips.

"Well," she asked, " are you gonna get up or not?"

"Be out in just a minute Liza," Libby answered.

She sat down on her bed and quickly pulled off her nightgown and pulled on her dress and apron.
She hurried outside the wagon and walked with Liza to the breakfast fire.

"Libby, here is a bowl of cornmeal mush for you. Have you had your breakfast Liza?" asked Mama.

"Yes Ma'am. I ate a long time ago. I've been up before the sun was even up. I heard Jesse came with the wild mare and her baby. I sure would like to see them. "

"Mama, would it be alright if we went to look at the wild mare?" asked Libby.

“Here is Jesse now, just coming for his breakfast. Better ask him if you can get close enough to see the mare.”

Jesse scooped up a bowl of mush from the cooking pot and poured milk and a bit of sugar on it then sat cross legged on the ground to eat his breakfast.

Libby clenched her hands together in front of her and walked very slowly to stand in front of Jesse.

“Jesse,” she asked softly, do you think we could see the mare and her baby?”

“She is still skittish and any little noise or movement can scare her and her colt. If the two of you want to see her you have to be very still and not move or talk while you are near her.”

“I promise Jesse. We will be so quiet you won’t know we’re there,” Libby answered.

“All right then, soon as I’m finished here we will slip quiet as we can back to the freight wagon. Will has her tied there just waiting until we can get shoes for her at the blacksmith’s.”

Libby and Liza walked quietly behind Jesse and slipped behind a big tree where they stood waiting as Jesse eased up toward the mare and her colt.

"Easy girl, easy now," he crooned in a low voice.

The mare tossed her head and whinnied then backed away as far as her rope would allow. Jesse kept walking toward her, talking softly as he came closer. When he reached her he lifted his arm up with palm outstretched, until he was able to touch the mare's head and then gently stroked her forehead. The mare whinnied and bent her head and sniffed Jesse's shirt, then made a low rumbling sound as she stood quietly.

Libby stood very still as she had promised until her feet felt numb and her back ached. She looked toward Liza, nodded and Liza nodded back. The two girls slipped softly away as they looked back one last time to watch the frisky colt dance around his mother.

"Whee! That was something wasn't it?" Liza said as the girls reached the wagons.

"I think Jesse is going to tame that wild mare pretty fast," Libby answered. "I sure like that baby and Jesse called it a colt so that means it's a boy.

"I guess so," said Liza. "Someday I hope to have a horse. Maybe someday in Oregon. Pa says our dreams will come true when we reach Oregon. I can't wait."

SODA SPRINGS

After three days they packed up the wagons and rolled out from Ft. Bridger. The Campbell family wagon now had the wheels repaired. The ox and mule teams were rested and they would soon reach Soda Springs.

The wild mare was roped to the back of the freight wagon and her baby followed along behind. Libby had promised Jesse to watch to see that the baby colt kept up with the wagons. She and Liza walked beside the freight wagon.Every time the baby colt strayed behind his mother, they reached out and tried to touch his sleek coat but the colt would scamper quickly ahead to reach his mother, before their hands could reach him.

When the wagons reached the Bear River Valley, the wagon train moved along the river bank on one side while on the other side of the river the mountains rose up rugged and steep. The valley floor was littered with lava rocks that made rough walking for the oxen and mules. Libby and Liza picked up pieces of lava and searched them for features that might give them answers as to what the lava had once covered.

"Papa says there were once volcanoes here and it left all these lava rocks," Libby said.

"Glad I wasn't here then. Imagine all the smoke and fire and loud old rumbling taking place then. I don't think it was a good place for anybody to have been here then. " Liza answered.

"No. Just thinking about it makes me shiver," Libby said.

The wagons rolled on until they reached a pine grove where they stopped for the night.

"Look up ahead," shouted Jesse as he came riding by on Princess. That"s the springs up ahead. Soda Springs they call em," he added as he rode away.

"Come on, Libby. Let's go see the springs," Liza said. Come on, Lazy Bones. Get a move on. We can catch up with Jesse."

The girls ran to follow Jesse and were soon joined by other children from the train.

"Oh, no," Libby cried out. "There is that awful, mean boy up ahead. Let's slow down for I don't want to catch up with him."

"Ah, come on Libby. You aren't gonna let that Martin brat scare you are you? Come on. We want to see what is going on."

" All right, but if Charlie Martin says a word to me you gotta help me punch him where he needs it."

“He won’t pay any attention to you. He’ll be all excited about the springs. Look! All the kids have stopped up ahead. Let’s hurry and get a look,” Liza said.

The girls reached the group of children and stood looking over several springs boiling up from the ground. They were cone shaped with an open top that was as much as three or four feet in diameter for the larger springs. The water shot up in the air then ran back into the cavity to shoot up again after a short time.

The girls walked closer to a big spring and could hear a sound like boiling water coming up from the spring. There was the smell of a gas coming from the cavity and the girls stepped back to keep from smelling it.

“I don’t like that smell,” Liza said.

“I don’t either,” Libby added. “But Papa says the water tastes like soda.”

“Want to give it a try?” asked Liza.

“Why not?” answered Libby. Lets go back to the wagons and get a bucket.”

The girls hurried away to the wagons and each got a tin pail for water. They ran back to the big spring and Libby saw Jesse and ran to him with her pail.

"Jesse, help me get some soda water. We want to make a drink."

"I don't know, Libby. This water tastes pretty strong. I just tasted some out of one of the springs. Some of them seem to be hot and some are cold. Let's find a cold one and maybe Mama can make some lemon soda."

"Over there Jesse" said Liza, pointing in the direction of a big spring.

"I'll give it a try. Let's have your buckets and I will fill em up if I can."

Jesse waited for the well to shoot up water then bent over to hold the pail under the spout until it was filled.

"Here's your water. Take it back to the wagons and see what Mama can make with it."

"Thanks, Jesse. You can have some too if you come back to the wagon," Libby said.

The girls hurried back to their wagons being careful not to spill the soda water.

"I'll take some to my Mama," Liza said. "See Ya!" Liza called as she hurried away to her wagon.

"Mama," Libby said as she reached the Campbell wagon. " I've got soda water from a spring. Will you help me make a soda drink?"

"Let me taste that water," Mama said. "Everyone has been saying you can make soda out of it."

She dipped a cup into the bucket of water and slowly drank a bit from it. She stood quietly, letting the water wash across her tongue then swallowed it.

"Seems to me it tastes a lot like the soda water we used to get at home. Let's put in some lemon syrup. I think we have some. I'll check my spice box in the wagon."

Mama brought out a jar that was half filled with lemon syrup. She carefully measured a few spoonfuls and poured it into the bucket of soda water.

"Now, let's stir this up and see if it tastes like lemon soda." she said.

She slowly poured the lemon soda mix into three cups then handed one to Nancy, one to Libby then picked up one for herself.

"All right girls, who wants to taste first?"

"I will answered Libby," and quickly touched her lips to the edge of her cup.

When the sweet soda taste reached her tongue she quickly drank from her cup.

"Slow down and take time to taste, " said Nancy.

"It's good!" called out Libby. "Just like real lemon soda." She finished her cup and went to the bucket for another.

"Wait Libby. Don't drink so fast. It may give you a tummy ache. Just one more cupful and then we need to save some for Jesse and Papa," Mama said.

"This is good Mama. Just like we used to get at the Finch's Market at home,"Nancy said.

"I"ll go tell Jesse to come get some" said Libby and dashed off to the springs again.

She could hear children's voices coming from the direction of the springs as she ran. There were sudden bursts of laughter then all went quiet. When she reached the group of children she edged her way to the front so that she could see. There was a spring with a small cone that reached up just a few inches and there was Charlie Martin on his knees bending over it. He had placed his cap over the small opening and was trying to hold it down on each side to keep the water from spouting up. For a few minutes all was quiet and Charlie looked up at the group with a satisfied smile.

"See, I told you I could keep that water from comin up."

His cap began to swell and puff out at the top. Charlie gritted his teeth and pressed down hard on each side of the cap. Suddenly a spout of water blew Charlie's cap high into the air sending Charlie straight back onto the ground..

The children laughed and shouted. "Yo, Charlie!"

A boy shouted, "Do it again, Charlie. Do it again."

"No sir, not me. There's a devil down there in that hole. I ain't gonna let him blow me up," and he ran after his cap, picked it up, beat it against his trousers then put it on his head and ran toward the wagons.

The children walked back toward the wagons and Libby called out to Jesse.

"Come taste the lemon soda, Jesse. It's really good. Mama is saving some for you."

"I'll come as soon as I take care of Princess," he said and climbed on her back.

***

At supper Papa and Jesse drank their share of lemon soda.

"I'll say," Papa said. This tastes pretty good. Most as good as the sodas we had at home."

"I'll have some more Papa if you don't want any more." Jesse said.

"Go ahead, I expect you got a powerful thirst herding the cattle through all these lava rocks today."

The family watched their supper fire die down and laughed about Charlie Martin getting his cap blown off the spring.

The next morning the air was crisp as Libby hugged her arms across her chest. Her jacket felt too thin to keep out the cold. She hurried to the breakfast fire and warmed her hands near the hot flames.

"Get your breakfast Libby. It will soon be time to move out. We want to be ready when the train starts," Mama said.

Libby ate breakfast then helped Mama wash and pack away the dishes. Nancy shook out the bedding and folded it and put it in the wagon. Just as they finished, Jesse came riding up on Princess.

"We're headed up past the spring called Steamboat Spring. They say it makes a sound just like a steamboat. Be watching for it once we get started."

Libby walked with Mama and Nancy. Little Ben sat on the wagon seat with Papa as they pulled away from their camp site and headed out toward Ft. Hall.

The wagons rolled along the Bear River. Libby was sorry to leave the Soda Springs campsite. It had been so much fun to watch the springs shoot up and to make lemonade out of the soda water.

"I'm going to watch for Steamboat Spring," Libby said. Jesse says that we can hear it before we get there."

"Hear that whistle?," Libby shouted to Nancy. "I think that is from the Steamboat Spring."

As the wagons traveled on the whistle became louder. Libby and Nancy watched the banks of Bear River and soon saw a spout of water rise up from a big rock near the bank. It reached up several feet. When they got closer they could see a red cone shape, probably made by the water that had boiled up over time.

"Do you hear that whistle Nancy?" Libby asked.

"Yes," Nancy answered. "See that small hole where steam comes out and there is vapor rising up over the hole? It looks like a puff of smoke. If I didn't know better I would think we were hearing the whistle from a steamboat."

"It sounds just like a steamboat doesn't it ?" Jesse called as he rode up on Princess. "I'll bet old Charlie won't be trying to stop that water from getting out. It comes out way too strong." The wagon train stopped and everyone watched the spring and listened to its loud whistle.

Captain Jamison called, "Wagons roll," and the wagon train moved ahead toward Ft. Hall.

When the wagon train neared Ft. Hall a group of Indians passed by. They were moving to a new camp. There were women on ponies with the family goods strapped on along with children who clung to their mothers. There were some Indian mothers with a papoose in a cradle board strapped to their backs. They moved slowly carrying all their worldly goods. The wagons stopped, making way for the ponies to pass by.

"Look at the beautiful moccasins that woman has," whispered Libby to Nancy.

"Yes, and look at the beadwork on the cradle board for that papoose," Nancy whispered back.

Jesse's wild mare nickered and pulled at her rope as far as it would stretch. As much as she pulled she couldn't reach the Indian ponies. Her baby colt ran toward his mother but could not get close to her as she pranced around in a half circle. She whinnied to the Indian ponies as long as they were near. After they had passed she blew through her nose then walked back to the end of the freight wagon and nuzzled her baby colt when he came trotting up to her.

Jesse rode by on Princess and called out to Libby, "Is the mare all right? I was afraid she would get loose and follow the Indian ponies."

"She's fine," Libby answered. "She wanted to follow them but the rope held her. Her colt stayed with her. They are both all right Jesse."

"Watch her for me. That rope could get tangled if she acts up."

"I'll watch her, " Libby said. "All the way to Ft. Hall."

"That shouldn't be too long. We should reach there before dark."

***

As they neared Ft. Hall they could see the white two story building with holes for rifles at the top. Around the fort was a tall wooden wall that enclosed houses and a store. At the top of the fort was a red flag with the letters HBC. This fort was owned by the Hudson's Bay Company, a British firm.

There were Indians and white fur traders, mountain men with furs to trade, some with Indian wives and children around the fort. There were immigrants with their wagons who had already reached Fort Hall. Outside the fort were old wagons and household goods of those who had abandoned them and taken pack horses for the rest of the trip.

Redtop halted the wagons and went inside the fort to check on camping places for the wagon train. They could hear shouts when he went inside.

"Hey, hey" and "Yippee," as he greeted some of his old friends.

Libby and Nancy sat in the wagon and Mama sat on the wagon seat with Papa and Little Ben while they waited for Redtop to return. Indians and trappers went in while others walked around outside the fort.
A man approached the wagon and walked up to Papa.

"My name's Baxter," he said. "I'm from Missouri headin for Oregon. The situation is that I've been hearin about is that it is a powerful rough journey across the Snake River and then on down the Columbia. Me and my family are thinkin of going with the California wagons. It can't be that bad. I think I would take dessert over mountains and dangerous rivers any day."

"Well, thanks for the information Mr. Baxter. I think my family and I will keep on with our trip to Oregon," Papa said.

"Good luck then and keep clear of trouble on the rivers," Mr. Baxter answered and walked away to another wagon.

Libby shivered as she sat huddled in the wagon. She reached out both hands and curled them tight.

"Did he say dangerous rivers?" she asked.

"I have heard the Snake River is swift and dangerous to cross. We will trust that Redtop and Captain Jamison will lead the way and keep us safe," Nancy answered.

Redtop and Captain Jamison returned to the wagons and the train moved out. They found a camping place that was about a mile from the fort.

After supper Libby, Nancy, Mama and Little Ben got ready to go back to the fort. Papa said that he and Jesse would take them in the wagon. They stopped the wagon outside the fort and entered the fort gate. They found a store where Mama bought some coffee and sugar. Papa and Jesse checked on fixing the rims for two of the freight wagon wheels.

Libby looked out in the fort yard and saw a young Indian girl. She had long black braids and wore a light buckskin dress with fringe that reached her ankles. The dress was decorated with beautiful colored beadwork. Libby smiled and the Indian girl smiled back.

"Hello," Libby said but the Indian girl just shook her head and turned away.

"I wish I could speak to her but I don't know her language," Libby sighed.

Mama, Libby, and Nancy walked back through the fort gate and stood waiting at the wagon for Papa and Jesse.

A man came up to them and asked Mama, "Going to Oregon ma'am?"

"Yes, we are on our way to Oregon," Mama answered.

"If I were you I would not even consider taking a wagon through to Oregon. There is too much rough trail and dangerous rivers. I wouldn't take my family that way. It's better to go on to California. The trail that way is easier."

"Thank you for the advice, mister. We are headed to Oregon," Mama answered.

Jesse and Papa came out of the fort gate and Jesse had a big smile.

Guess who I just talked to?" he asked. "Running Wolf, an

Indian boy. He said he would help me train my wild mare. Captain Jamison said we would be here a couple more days while the cattle rest up. Tomorrow morning I am going to bring in the mare and he said he would help me. He says he has trained wild horses before."

"That's good Jesse," Mama said. " Captain Jamison may need Princess and it will be good if you can have a horse of your own.

"Can I watch you train her?" Libby asked."

"Don't know any reason why not if Papa and Mama says so."

"Only if Nancy will stay with you Libby. If she will watch over you, you have my permission to go back to the fort and watch," Mama said.

Libby asked, " Will you come with me Nancy?"

"Sure I will. I'd like to see how the Indian boy trains a horse."

After breakfast the next morning Jesse led the wild mare toward Ft. Hall. Libby and Nancy walked beside them. The baby colt jumped up and down in the dusty trail then ran after his mother.

When they reached the fort the Indian boy came out to meet them. He wore leather leggings and a dark leather buckskin shirt. His hair was done up in a long braid that hung down his back.

"Hello," he called. "I see you brought mare."

"Here she is," answered Jesse.

"Bring her to the corral in back. I will help you ride your spotted mare."

"Jesse," Libby whispered. "That Indian boy speaks English."

"Yes," Jesse answered. "His family lives here at the fort. His father is a scout for the Hudson's Bay Company. Running Wolf learned to speak English here."

Jesse led the mare to a a corral enclosed with long poles.

Running Wolf took a horsehair rope and tied the baby colt to a large wooden log. "Baby will stay safe here," he said.

He walked up to the mare and asked, "What is the mare's name?"

"She doesn't have one yet," Jesse answered.

"I'll call her Gasa. It means wing in Shoshone. I am Shoshone. I give the mare a Shoshone name.

Gasa runs fast like she has wings."

"She can run fast all right, " Jesse answered. "I don't want her to get loose. I probably couldn't catch her. Even if I rode the Captain's horse Princess I wouldn't be able to catch her."

Running Wolf led Gasa inside the corral. He slowly led her around the enclosed corral. Gasa pranced and blew from her nostrils until Running Wolf shortened the rope in his hand and her head could not move far from him. All the while he talked softly to her, his voice never rising, speaking Shoshone words to her.

After the mare started following quietly Running Wolf tied her to the corral fence. He took off his leather shirt and held it in his hands, walking slowly toward her. Reaching the shirt out in front of him he let her sniff it then slowly lifted it up over her back and slid it down her sides. She moved to the side as far as her rope would allow and gave a snort at the shirt. Running Wolf took the shirt away and brought it back again and again until Gasa stood still.

"Time to ride," Running Wolf spoke softly to Jesse.

He leaned his body next to Gasa standing quietly for a moment, resting his arms across her back, then quickly sprang up and across her back. Gasa gathered her legs together and tried to spring up in the air but the rope held her.

"Loose the rope." He called to Jesse.

Jesse quickly loosened the rope and Gasa exploded up off the ground. She rose high in the air then came down hard to the ground again. Running Wolf gripped her sides with his legs and hugged his body low over her back. Gasa jumped again and again but Running Wolf stayed on her back. Gasa stopped bucking then ran around the corral .

"Look at that mare run!" shouted Jesse.

"Look at Running Wolf staying on her back," Nancy replied.

Running Wolf rode around the corral until Gasa slowed down and started blowing through her nostrils. He pressed her sides with his knees to guide her to the left or to the right. When she began to move very slowly and her glossy brown and white spotted sides were damp with sweat, Running Wolf brought her over to Jesse and handed him the rope that was tied around Gasa's neck.

"Lead Gasa around the coral to cool down," he said to Jesse.

Jesse led the mare around the corral until she was breathing normally and her coat was starting to dry off.

"Take Gasa back to camp and bring her tomorrow. We will ride again.

Jesse, Nancy and Libby walked Gasa back to the wagon train. Jesse watered and fed Gasa and her baby while Libby and Nancy helped Mama with supper.

"Gasa is a good name for the mare. She runs like she has wings," said Jesse at supper.

"Do you think you can ride her Jesse?" asked Libby

"Maybe, after Running Wolf rides her again," Jesse answered.

While the family sat around the supper camp fire talking about Gasa and her colt, Liza walked up near the fire.

Libby could see that she had been crying and asked, "Liza, what is wrong? Are you hurt?"

She ran to Liza and put her arm around her shoulders.

"No, nothin like that. I'm not hurt. I just hurt inside."

"Nancy jumped up from her seat and ran to Liza. "Liza, can we help you?"

"Nobody can help cause Pa has made up his mind. We're

not goin to Oregon. We're taking the trail from here to California. No matter what Ma and I say he won't change his mind. The big talkers around here have persuaded him to go to California. They say it is easier. I don't want to go. I want to stay with you Libby," she said hanging her head low.

"Liza," Libby said. "I sure will miss you. If your Pa won't change his mind I suppose we will have to say a sad goodby. I surely wish you weren't going but guess you have to go with your family. Maybe you can come with us tomorrow and watch Jesse and Running Wolf train Gasa. We'll make our last day together a fun day if that's alright with you Jesse?"

"That's a good idea if your Pa and Ma agree. You are welcome to come with us Liza," answered Jesse.

After Liza went back to her wagon, the family talked about the people who had decided to leave the train to Oregon and take the route to California.

"We will sure miss those folks," Mama said.

"Yes, we will and we are lucky that Captain Jamison is going on to Oregon with us, " Papa said.

***

The next morning after breakfast Libby, Nancy and Liza

were ready for Jesse when he brought Gasa and her colt to the family wagon. Mama handed Nancy a pail of food for lunch time.

"Here is some bread, bacon and some dried apples for your lunch," she said.

"Libby, fill the water barrel and every other thing that can hold water today, " Papa called. We will be traveling over some dry country tomorrow."

"I will Papa when we get back."

"Make sure you do because the chances of finding water tomorrow are not good, Captain Jamison says."

"Jesse," Liza asked. "When are you going to name Gasa's baby? I think he needs a name."

"We have to find the right name soon Liza. Got any good names you can think of?"

"The only names I can think of today are sad names. I don't know a single thing about California but guess we are sure enough going to go there tomorrow," Liza said.

"Liza, maybe we will see you again if we ever visit California or if your folks come to Oregon someday," Nancy said.

"Maybe," Liza answered. "But it bein so far it ain't likely we ever will."

"Let's just say we will see each other again, Liza," said Libby. "And let's say we will and have fun today," Libby said.

***

Running Wolf was waiting for them at the fort and took Gasa's lead rope and headed for the pole corral behind the fort. Jesse tied the colt to a log again and he nickered for his mother as she was led away.

Running Wolf tied Gasa to a corral pole and took off his leather shirt. He held it out to the mare again and she sniffed it and tossed her head. He drew it back then forward until she stood still. He slid the shirt across her back and down her sides then lay against her back until Gasa was quiet. He then gave a quick leap onto her back. She pulled back on the rope and pulled her legs together to get ready to buck. Running Wolf was quick and pulled the rope, loosening it from its pole. Gasa jumped into the air and ran around the corral fence. Running Wolf held on tight. "Yee-ha!" he yelled and waved one hand high in the air. He rode her until she stopped, then slid off and led her to Jesse.

Gasa began to tire and slowed her pace as she trotted around the corral. Running Wolf stayed on her back until she stopped then slid off and led her to Jesse.

"Gasa needs to cool down. She worked hard." Running Wolf said as he handed her rope to Jesse.

Libby brushed back the loose hair that had escaped her braids. "I sure wish I had a cold drink of water," she said.

"I suppose you could get one inside the fort. You have my permission to go if you want," Nancy said

"Want to go too Liza?" Libby asked.

"No, I want to stay here and watch Gasa. Bring us some water though."

"How am I supposed to bring water. I don't have a water bucket," Libby answered.

"Here," said Nancy, taking the things out of the lunch pail and wrapping them in the old towel Mama had put with it.

Libby took the empty pail and stood looking toward the fort for a moment. It seemed far off and a bit scary to walk past all the Indians and campers outside. She took a deep breath and ran toward the fort making the dust fly from under her feet.

"Where you going little gal?" a man called out from a wagon. Libby hurried ahead never looking back. Never answering the man. She had just reached the big gate and was walking inside the cool, dark fort when someone called out from behind her.

"Hey, I got something for you. "

Libby turned around and saw the pest, Charlie Martin, behind her. Now what did that mean boy want? She was mad and she stomped her feet and put her hands on her hips. Her face was red and sweaty from the hot sun and loose strands of hair from her braids fell around her face.

"What is it you want Charlie Martin?" she asked.

" I got something here I think you might want. I found it back on the trail and I know it belongs to you Campbells. I heard my Ma say you was making it for Jesse. "

"Making it for Jesse?" Libby shouted. " You found the leather jacket didn't you? All this time you've been keeping it for yourself. Well it doesn't belong to you. I want it back. We wanted to make it for Jesse so he wouldn't be so sad about his mare, Maggie. You remember Maggie don't you and what happened to her? It was all because of you."

"I know it. I am sorry. I was goin to give it back when we got to Oregon but Pa says we are joinin up with the wagons going to California so here it is. I won't be seeing you in Oregon."

Charlie tossed the old pillow case into Libby's arms. She slowly opened the end and saw the leather sleeves of the jacket. She pulled them out and spread the jacket against her. Seeing that the jacket was all there and in perfect condition she slowly raised her eyes to look at Charlie who stood with his hands at his sides looking sad.

"Thanks Charlie," Libby said. "I am glad you found it and decided to give it back. I hope you like California and can be nice to people there. They will like you better if you are."

"Yeah, I know," Charlie said and turned around and ran from the fort.

***

Libby filled the empty pail with water, all the time keeping the old pillow case with the jacket inside tucked under her arm. She hurried outside the fort gate with the pail in one hand and the pillow case held tight in the other hand.

When she reached the corral she hurried to Nancy and with a soft voice said, " Nancy look. Look at what I have. It's Jesse's leather jacket," she said, handing the pillowcase to Nancy.

"Oh, this is wonderful Libby," said Nancy holding the jacket up in front of her. "Where did you find it? Was it inside the fort?"

"Was it Libby?" asked Liza.

"No, it wasn't. Mean, old Charlie Martin had it all this time. He said he was going to give it to me in Oregon but now his Pa is going to California so he gave it to me at the fort."

"Charlie must be getting soft on you, Libby," Liza teased.

"Well, I think it was good of him to give it back to us," Nancy said.

"I wouldn't count on it any," Liza said. "An ole pole cat don't changed none if you ask me. I sure don't need that pest going along with us to California."

"He might want a friend right now and if you treat him nice he may be nice too. You can always try, " Nancy said.

"He can show me first," said Liza. "I don't expect nothin from him but meanness."

"Well, let's hope he does better," said Nancy. "Now lets have our lunch with a cold drink of water."

***

After lunch Jesse rode the spotted mare around and around the corral. Running Wolf leaned on the corral fence and watched until Gasa began to slow her pace.

"Time to go," Running Wolf said. " Gasa is tired and you can now ride her. Ride every day. Keep working her."

Liza and Libby chatted all the way back to the campground. Jesse led Gasa and Nancy tucked the old pillow case with the jacket into the lunch pail away from Jesse's eyes. When they reached the wagons Liza stayed near the Campbell wagon talking to Libby until supper time.

"I hope you have a wonderful trip to California," Libby said.

"I don't expect it to be wonderful. You won't be there. I will miss you so much Libby," Liza said.

She wrapped her arms around Libby's shoulders and Libby reached up and hugged her friend. The girls stood holding each other and sobbing softly. Then Liza turned quickly and ran toward her family's wagon.

Libby called, "Take care Liza."

Liza called back as she ran through the growing darkness, "You too Libby."

Libby sank down on the wagon tongue. She lay her head in her lap and wrapping her arms around her ears, blotted out the sounds of the campers bringing in the livestock and preparing the evening meal. The night was black when Mama came to the wagon and touched Libby's shoulder to tell her it was supper time.

The family ate their meal quietly thinking of the friends that were leaving for California.

Mama spoke to Libby, "I am sorry you are losing your friend Liza. Go ahead and go to bed.

Nancy and I will clean up the dishes."

Libby walked back to the wagon. The whole time she dressed in her nightgown she felt she was missing something. What had she overlooked? Something didn't seem right. She sat on the edge of her bed for a little while but couldn't remember anything. With a sigh she lay down on her bed and was soon asleep.

***

Early the next morning the wagon train moved out headed away from Fort Hall. They would travel over dry, dusty country to reach a place to cross the Snake river called the Island Crossing. The hot sun beat down on the dry sand and the wagons stirred up dust that filled the air until the oxen pulling the wagons could hardly be seen. Libby slowly pulled her feet through the deep sand as she tried hard to keep up with Nancy and Mama.

"It is such a hot day," Mama said as she stopped to wipe her face and take a quick rest. "Who would think the heat and dust could give so much trouble. I am ready to stop for nooning already and I know from the sun's position it isn't nearly noon."

"I don't care if it isn't noon. I am ready to stop," said Libby.

"We must keep going for awhile," Mama said. "We don't want to be so long on this trip that we get caught in the snow when we reach the mountains."

Libby pulled her sunbonnet farther down on her head and hid her face inside the deep sides. I could use some water right now,"she said.

"We will get a drink when we stop at noon," Mama answered.

When the wagons finally stopped for nooning it was a dry camp. There was no spring or river nearby. Papa and Jesse hurried to the water barrel on the side of the wagon to get water for the animals. They carried water in buckets to the oxen and mules.

As Jesse started to fill another bucket he shouted "We're out of water. This old spigot is turned as far as it will go and not another drop comes out," he shouted.

Papa hurried to Jesse's side.

"Surely not," he said. "We just filled it last night."

He tipped the barrel down to let out a few more drops of water then pushed it back up.

"It's empty all right. It could have a leak I suppose. Libby did you fill this up last night?"

Libby stood with her head down. Now she remembered what she couldn't think of before she went to bed. She forgot to fill the water barrel like Papa had told her.

"So, did you fill the water barrel Libby?" Papa asked.

"No Papa, I forgot," Libby whispered.

"Now we're on this hot dusty trail and we have no water. It will be a thirsty day for you my daughter, and for all the rest of us as well."

"I didn't mean to Papa," Libby pleaded.

"The water supply has to come first. Without it we will die. It was your job to fill the barrel. We all have a responsibility to each other if we want to survive this trip. You have failed yours

Libby. You have let us down and now we will all have to suffer," Papa said and quickly turned his back to Libby and walked away.

Libby climbed inside the wagon and lay down on her bed. She knew that she had done a very bad thing. What would they do without water? Burrowing her face in her pillow she sobbed until she grew tired. She finally got up from her bed and climbed out of the wagon to see everyone eating a cold lunch of beans and buffalo jerky. There was a plate filled waiting for her. She looked around at the family members but nobody would look at her. They turned their dusty heads away and kept on eating their cold food.

"I'm sorry," Libby said. "I didn't mean to forget the water."

"Jesse looked directly at her and said in an angry voice, "You sure picked a sorry time to do it. I don't know when I have wished more for a drink of water."

Libby reached for her plate and carried it away from the family group to a dusty spot beside the wagon. She sat down on the ground and began eating. The moist beans tasted good and for a while her mouth didn't feel so dry. When the beans were gone she chewed on the buffalo jerky. It stuck in her mouth and just wouldn't slide down her dry throat. Feeling that she was choking, Libby coughed and spit the pieces out of her mouth on to the dry, dusty ground. The tears begin to move down her dusty cheeks and feeling awfully miserable she set her plate down, folded her arms around her head, and rested it on her bent knees. She sobbed for the mistake she had made and she sobbed because she was so thirsty. She could hear her own loud sobs but no one else seemed to hear them. Nobody came to put a hand on her shoulder or give her a hug. No one in the family seemed to care. They didn't even seem to know she was there.

***

The dishes rattled as Mama and Nancy put things away. Libby lifted her head when Papa started the wagon and jumped up and ran after it. Mama and Nancy walked ahead and Little Ben rode on the wagon seat beside Papa. Nobody waited for Libby. She ran through the dust and it came puffing up to her dry mouth as she ran to catch them.

The day dragged on. Libby was all alone. Mama and Nancy stayed ahead, Little Ben rode in the wagon, and Jesse was back on Gasa herding the cattle. Libby was so thirsty but the water barrel was empty. "It's all because of me," she whispered to herself.

***

The day was long and weary and when the wagons circled for the night camp the travelers were again without water. The dry camp was a disappointment to everyone. The thirsty oxen bawled for a drink. They could be heard all around the camp. The tired and thirsty mules bowed their heads with no energy left to stomp away the flies that settled over them.

Libby sat down on the wagon tongue. She was too tired and thirsty to go any further. Her lips were swollen and cracked from the hot dry air and no water. She looked up to see Mama coming with the grease bucket.

"Libby, smooth some of this grease over your lips and it will relieve them from being so sore," She said.

"Grease, Mama? Black, smelly grease? I don't think I want that on my mouth."

"It's the best that we have. With no water tonight, your lips will get even more sore. Here, I'll help you, " and she stuck her finger into the grease bucket then smeared the grease across Libby's lips.

"Mama," Libby said, starting to cry again, "I really did forget the water but not on purpose. I forget because I was sad about Liza leaving the train."

"I know Libby, but we always have to think of our chores

first. It may mean our very lives if things don't get done. Remember that Libby."

"I will Mama. I will."

ISLAND CROSSING

The wagons stopped on the edge of the Island Crossing at the Snake River. The water was deep and swift, running between two islands and the far shore. Libby stared down into the water.

Oh, if we had just had some of this water to drink when we were so thirsty she thought. If I had just remembered to fill the water barrel then everyone wouldn't be so angry with me. She looked around at the wagons gathering on the bank waiting to cross the river. The water looked dangerous. Captain Jamison had hired an Indian guide to show them the safest way to cross.

"We need to caulk the wagons with tar and rags to keep the water out," Papa said.

"Get started on it right now. We want to be ready when it comes our turn to cross."

Things were moved away from the edges of the wagon. Mama, Nancy and Libby soaked pieces of old clothes in tar and pushed them up against the inside edges of the wagon until every crack was filled.

Jesse rode Gasa, driving the cattle to the river bank. They stood bawling and milled around the water's edge, restless and fearing the rushing water.

"Get the cattle to follow the Indian guide," Papa called.

An Indian on a big black horse rode into the water heading for the first island. Jesse rode Gasa up and down the river bank urging the cattle forward. The cattle pushed away refusing to enter the water. As they milled about, a small calf was pushed over the side of the riverbank into the water. Its mother jumped into the water to reach her baby. Another and another followed until the whole herd was swimming across the river.

Jesse and Will tied Gasa's baby with rope and put him in the freight wagon.

"Why do you have to tie up Gasa's baby?" Libby asked Jesse.

"He's too young to swim the river. He couldn't make it. This way he can have a ride. Get ready to cross," Jesse called.

Mama, Nancy, Little Ben and Libby climbed into the wagon. Libby's legs trembled as she sat on her bed holding tight to a wagon bow . She couldn't see but she could hear what was going on outside.

"Get up Toby. Get in there Tucker. Go Prince. Ho Barney. " Papa called to the mules, urging them into the water behind the

Indian guide.

The wagon lurched forward into the river water. It was swift and Papa urged the mules ahead. They reached the first island, then the second. They were ready to cross the last stretch of river.

"Ho Toby. Get going Tucker," Papa shouted to the mules as they started across the last deep stretch of water.

When the wagon tilted up as it climbed the river bank Libby dared to loosen her hold on the wagon bow and peek out back . The wide stretch of water was behind them at last.

The wagon stopped and Libby scrambled out and followed Mama, Nancy and Little Ben to the edge of the river. On the opposite bank Jesse was riding Gasa and was ready to start across the river beside the freight wagon on the down side. Will was riding Princess on the upper side of the oxen. They would try to keep the oxen moving forward and not let them drift down stream The oxen pulled the wagon into the water. They followed the Indian guide to the first island then the second. They started across the last stretch of water. Will rode close to the lead oxen.

"Get in there Baldy," he shouted.

The big ox struggled against the swift water then started

drifting down river with the current.

"Get in there. Hi, hi, hi!," Will screamed, trying to catch hold of the ox yoke.

The powerful current caught the team in its swift rush downstream and the heavy freight wagon tipped toward the water. The chains that fastened it to the ox team tightened. It teetered for a moment then righted back with a jerk.

Jesse on the downstream side of the wagon pulled on Gasa's reins to urge her out of the way of the heavy wagon. Gasa was frightened and plunged into a deep hole. She reared up out of the water and Jesse flew off her back. He struggled to keep his head out of the swift water and get away from the freight wagon.

"Jesse!" Libby screamed and ran along the river bank watching as her brother clung to the wagon chain to keep his head above water.

"Catch hold Jesse, " called Papa as he tossed a rope across the water.

"I"m caught," Jesse shouted.

The Indian guide rode back into the river urging his horse through the water to Jesse's side. With a swift movement, he thrust out a knife and slashed Jesse's pant leg, releasing it from the wagon chain. He reached down for Jesse's arm and lifted him up onto the black horse. They plunged back across the water to the riverbank.

Will struggled with the oxen. The team slowly edged toward shore. At last the heavy freight wagon reached the riverbank.Libby went flying toward Jesse.

"Jesse, are you all right? Are you hurt Jesse?" she sobbed.

Mama was beside Jesse who lay on the ground. She gently pulled away the rest of his pant leg. Her face turned pale as she looked at the broken bone sticking up from his leg. She wiped his forehead with a damp cloth and said, "We will fix you up son. You will be fine."

"Tears rolled down Jesse's cheeks from the pain of his broken leg and the terrible fright of the rushing water determined to sweep him away.

"Gasa? Would somebody get her?" Jesse pleaded.

Papa leaned over Jesse, "Gasa is safe. She's a strong little mare and made it across."

Jesse was moved to the family wagon and lay on Libby's bed. Papa made a wooden splint from two flat boards and bound them with strips of leather cut from a buffalo skin. They would wait by the river for the wagon train behind them. A doctor who was traveling with that train could look at Jesse's broken leg.

"I brought you some cold water Jesse," Libby said. She stood inside the wagon looking down at her brother.

"Don't need any water Libby "find Gasa and take care of her."

"I can't Jesse. I don't know how. Maybe Will can do it," Libby answered.

"You have to find her and take care of her. Will doesn't have time. There is nobody else to

help. She'll run away if somebody doesn't take care of her. You have to Libby. You have to take care of her and her baby."

Libby looked down at her brother's face. She wanted to earn his approval.

"Maybe I can try. Would Will help me do you think?"

"Maybe this evening before it gets dark, he might. You can ask him."

Libby climbed down from the wagon. The other wagons had now left and only the two Campbell wagons were camped by the side of the river. Indians were trading fish to Mama and Nancy. Will had Gasa's baby out of the wagon and he was calling for his mother. Papa was taking care of the mules.

Libby followed Will as he unyoked the tired oxen and lay the big ox yokes on the ground.

"Will, would you help me?" she asked.

Will kept working, not hearing what she said.

"Will! Will!" she called and ran after Will and took hold of his arm as he lifted the last ox yoke down to the ground.

Will turned around in surprise. "I wondered what that was on my arm and it's you Little Miss. You're not in trouble agin are ye?"

"Not this time," Libby answered. But Will, I need your help awfully bad."

"And how so, Missy?"

" Jesse is hurt and he can't take care of his mare. He wants me to find her and I need some help. Do you know where Gasa is?"

"Yep, I got that little mare all caught and tied right down by the river. Go tell your brother we have her and then come back and we will bring her up to the freight wagon to her baby for the night."

"I'll tell him Will. I don't know who's going to ride her now that Jesse can't."

"Why he is figure'n on you ridin her I'm guessin."

"Me, Will? Me ride that wild mare? I rode Maggie just a little while. I don't know how to ride a wild mare."

"Peers to me you better get ta learn'n pretty quick."

"I'll tell Jesse you found her ," Libby said and ran back to the family wagon.

She climbed into the wagon and looked down at Jesse sleeping on her bed.

"All right Jesse," she whispered, "You sleep now. I will ride Gasa. I promise."

The morning sun sparkled on the river water. Libby stood on the bank and watched as wagons from the train that had followed them came across the river. The doctor in this train could help Jesse. It was evening when Papa came to the wagon with Dr. Langston. He looked at Jesse's leg and said that it was set right and that he couldn't do any better himself. He said that it would take time to heal and Jesse would have to keep his weight off it for some time. Papa made some crutches out of wood so that Jesse could move about.

At the supper campfire Jesse sat on the ground with his legs extended. Mama, Nancy and Libby all did their best to get the things he needed.

Little Ben hugged his big brother and said, "I'll let you blow my willow whistle Jesse."

Jesse ran his hands through Little Ben's mop of blond hair and answered, "Thanks Ben. You keep your whistle safe because when we reach Oregon you will want to blow it as hard as you can to celebrate."

After supper, Jesse called to Libby. "All right Libby. Time to go check on Gasa. Let's go see how she is doing."

Jesse reached for his homemade crutches and swung himself forward. It was not easy for him but he was determined. He followed Libby to a small willow near the freight wagon and there was Gasa and her colt.

"Hello, Gasa, " Jesse crooned as he bent his head down against the little mare's neck.

Gasa nickered softly.

"Now Libby," he said, "come close and let her smell you."

Libby stood in front of Gasa. She sniffed her then backed

away.

"Whoa little girl. It's just Libby. She won't hurt you," Jesse said and moved closer.

"Now Libby, come here and reach out slowly to touch her. No quick moves, just slowly and gently."

Libby reached out for Gasa's forehead and gently smoothed it with her hand.

She spoke softly, "Hello Gasa you are so pretty. Nice Gasa. You can fly like the wind," she said, her voice ever so soft.

***

Libby and Jesse worked morning and evening while they camped for two more days.. Jesse would stand on his crutches talking softly while Libby smoothed the mare's forehead and neck. By the time the wagons were ready to pull out, Gasa would let Libby stand very close against her shoulders and smooth her hands across her back.

"We will get Will to help you up on her back tomorrow," Jesse told Libby.

"I'll try, Jesse but I'm scared."

"Don't be scared. She can sense it and she will throw you

off."

"All right, I will just make myself try."

The wagons traveled on through the long day and caught up with the main train at last where they had stopped at a camping place for the night.

The next day Nancy rode one of the Conners' mares and helped herd the cattle now that Jesse couldn't do it. She came to the family wagon with her dark hair mostly grey with dust, and her face streaked with dirt.

"I can't wait to get some of this dust off," she said.

"I'll help with supper," Libby said.

She got out Mama's spider and iron cooking pot. While Mama cooked the salmon and

warmed the beans, she got out the tin plates and cups. She worked beside Mama quietly. Mama looked up at last and said, "Thank you Libby."

Libby felt warm inside because Mama had noticed that she was trying to help. Maybe Mama was no longer angry with her for not filling the water barrel.

***

The wagon train reached the foot of the Blue Mountains

and stopped for the night.Libby visited Gasa every day and Will promised to help her ride the mare. When camp was made and supper was over, Libby and Jesse slowly walked beside Will to the freight wagon where Gasa was tied. Her baby was suckling his Mama's warm milk. Jesse swung on his crutches until he could reach out and smooth Gasa's neck. She sniffed his shirt and whinnied softly.

"All right my girl, tonight you are going to give Libby a ride. Be a good girl and give her a fine ride."

"Now Libby, it's time to mount up."

Libby stood back. Her legs trembled and she pressed her hands together to keep them from shaking.

"I don't know Jesse, maybe we should wait a day."

"No, she knows you now and will let you get on her back. Come on and let Will boost you up."

Libby was afraid. She didn't want to get on the mare's back. She hung back, not moving.

"Jesse, I don't think I can. I know I promised but I'm scared."

"Come over here and forget about being scared."

Slowly Libby inched toward Gasa and reached out to touch her forehead. Gasa flung her head up and gave a loud snort. Libby stepped back then moved forward again.

Will stood behind her and reached his big hands around her waist and said, “Up you go Little Miss,” and put her on Gasa’s back.

Will loosened the rope that tied Gasa and led her past the freight wagon. Libby stared to relax and clung to Gasa’s mane. Just as she did Gasa arched her back with a quick buck and Libby went flying to the ground.

“You all right Libby?” Jesse called out.

Will reached down and pulled Libby up from the ground. “Get up and dust yerself off. Bein throwed is jest part of horse ridin.”

Libby started to cry. “I can’t do this Jesse,” she sobbed.

“Yes you can. Come on. Walk up slowly and get back on Gasa’s back. You can do it. You can ride her. You promised.”

Libby wiped her wet checks with her fists and brushed off her skirt and slowly walked up to Gasa again.

“Ready fer another try?” Will asked.

Libby nodded her head and Will lifted her up on Gasa’s

back.

Will took the lead rope and Libby gripped the mare's sides with her legs and gently gripped her mane. Gasa walked over the sandy ground and Libby stayed on her back and began to enjoy her smooth stride. Will led her up the trail for a time and then back again to the freight wagon. Libby slid off the mare's back.

"See, you can ride Gasa, Libby," Jesse said.

"I did didn't I? I think she knows me now."

***

At bedtime Libby lay in her bed listening to an owl's call. She wasn't afraid of that scary sounding old owl. She could ride a wild mare.

The next morning the wagons were made ready to climb the mountains. Wheels were greased, wagon tires were tightened and things put in order inside. There was not much to throw away now to lighten the load. They had only the the things that were absolutely necessary to reach Oregon.

Libby helped Mama pack away the dishes and bedding and Papa greased the wagon wheels. Nancy was riding Ladyfair, waiting for Mason to come help her with the cattle.

“The cattle are going to be hard to keep together when we get into those big trees up on the mountain. Mama can drive the mules and I will help you if you have trouble keeping them together,” Papa said.

The first climb was steep and rocky. The wagon wheels skidded over the rocks and the wagons rocked from side to side. Libby stepped over big rocks and hurried to walk under the trees where evergreen needles covered the ground and made a soft pillow for her feet.

“Yah-hoo-hoo.” came a call.

Libby stopped and listened as it echoed through the mountains. She put her hands around her mouth and answered the call.

“Yah-hoo-hoo.”

Her voice echoed back to her again.

“Libby I need your help,” Mama called. “Papa must ride Gasa and help Nancy and Mason with the cattle. They are getting lost in the trees. You need to watch Ben. He can’t ride in the wagon. Jesse has to ride there and we must lighten the load. Ben will have to to walk with you.”

“Papa will ride Gasa, Mama? ”

"We have no other horse to ride and Nancy called for Papa to come help."

Libby helped Little Ben down from the wagon and took his hand.

"We'll walk around the big rocks Ben so hold my hand tight and you won't fall."

Mama sat on the wagon seat and called to the mules as they struggled up the steep mountain.

"Get up Toby. Ho Tucker," she shouted.

"Get in there Baldy. Hep, hep,"Will called out as he urged the oxen ahead.

"Whoa," Mama called as one of the wagon wheels caught on a large rock and the mules struggled to pull it forward.

Will came to look at the back wagon wheel and said, "Not much chance getting over this here rock. Them mules can't pull it over. We gotta get some help. I'll get Captain Jamison."

"Got some trouble there have you?" Captain Jamison asked when he rode up on his mare Sadie.

"We need to get past this big old boulder. The mules ain't goin nowhere till it's out of the way." Will said.

Captain Jamison climbed down from Sadie and looked at the stuck wagon wheel. "Seems it might be best to back up the wagon and pull it around the rock."

"Them ole oxen are pretty close behind but I'll see if I can back em up a bit," Will answered.

Will prodded and shouted until the oxen inched back. He grabbed the brake and pushed hard as the wagon started rolling backward.

"Woo-ooo-ah," he shouted and the oxen put their giant shoulders against their yokes holding the wagon steady.

Will and Captain Jamison eased the mules backward until the wagon wheel rolled back. Will put his shoulder to the back of the wagon and pushed and Captain Jamison drove the mules forward around the big boulder.

"Good job," Captain Jamison said. He mounted Sadie and rode away.

Mama pushed back the hair that had come loose from her bun, put her hands on her hips, and stood staring at the wagon. Slowly, with a determined shrug of her shoulders, she climbed up to the wagon seat.

A sound of swishing branches came from the dark trees. Libby stopped and pulled Little Ben close to her and tightened her trembling arms around him. It might be a big bear coming out of there she thought. Could she run with Little Ben for the wagon? She was too scared to move. Little Ben felt Libby's tight arms and begin to cry.

"Hush Ben", Libby warned and and held him even tighter as she bent her head down and whispered, "Shush, Ben," and stood very still listening.

The sound of crashing limbs came from the trees. Out rushed Gasa with reins from her bridle dragging the ground.

"Gasa! Woah, Gasa!" Libby shouted and ran up the mountain behind the mare. Gasa swerved around the wagons and ran on.

"Come back Libby. You can't catch her, " Mama shouted.

Jesse leaned out from the back of the wagon and called to Libby, "Her colt is tied to the freight wagon. She will come back to him."

"What about Papa? He was going to ride Gasa."

"She must have run away before he could get a chance to ride her," Jesse answered.

"Papa will find us and Gasa will come back for her baby." Mama said.

***

The mules climbed up the mountain slowly stepping over fallen limbs and loosening rocks that rolled back toward the freight wagon. Will had to urged the tired oxen ahead keeping them away.

Gasa called to her baby with a loud whinny. The little colt struggled to get loose from the rope that tied him to the back of the freight wagon. He called to his mother with a short, little whinny. It was enough to reach Gasa's ears and she came bounding down the mountain. The colt nuzzled his mother and she whinnied softly to him.

"Libby," Jesse said .` "Take her reins and tie her up to the freight wagon."

"I will, Jesse if I can get close to her.

She walked slowly and spoke softly then reached out and touched the mare's forehead. She gently smoothed her hand down her neck and caught the reins, then tied them to the back of the freight wagon.

"Now, little girl. You will be all right. Your baby is here."

Jesse walked with his crutches to help Libby calm the mare. He stroked her shoulder and talked to her. Gasa turned her head and nuzzled Jesse's shirt and gave a low rumbling whinny.

"I see you got that blasted mare," Papa called as he came out from the dark trees and up to the wagons.

"What happened Papa?" Libby asked.

"Did she throw you Papa?" Jesse asked.

"Throw me? She ran away before I could get close enough to get on her. That little piece of horse flesh is worthless if we can't ride her."

"She got scared Papa. She doesn't know you. I can ride her and Libby can too."

"Then Libby better get herself up on her back and help out Nancy and Mason. The cattle are scattered everywhere. We've got to round them up or lose 'em.

Libby stood still and her mouth flew open in surprise.

"You can do it Libby," Jesse said. "I've trained her to find the cows and chase them home."

"But Jesse, I have never rounded up cows before. What if I fall off?"

"You can give it a try if you want," Papa said. It isn't easy riding through this timber. Better keep low so a limb doesn't knock you off.

Libby reached out to touch Gasa. "Will you let me ride you little girl?" she whispered softly. Gasa nudged her shoulder and gave a soft whinny.

Are you up to it Libby?" Papa asked.

Libby stood for a moment then slowly nodded her head.

"Let her have her way and she'll find the cows. Stick low on her back and she will bring them back to the main herd. I know you can ride her Libby, " Jesse said.

Papa boosted Libby up on the mare's back and she took the reins. Gasa whirled around and made a dash for the woods. Libby clung tight to her back leaning forward to stay low as they rode through the trees.

Gasa saw two young heifers in some short bushes and dashed after them running them through the woods until they reached the main herd .

Nancy was riding behind the herd moving them ahead. "What are you doing riding Gasa?" she called out to Libby.

"Helping find the strays," Libby shouted.

The herd started to separate and Nancy dashed away to bring them together and didn't wait for answer.

Gasa found strays and Libby clung to her back, leaving the

reins loose to let the mare find her own way. Gasa kept finding one cow and then another, running them back to the main herd. Finally there were no more strays. Libby rode behind the main herd . Nancy and Mason rode on opposite sides of the herd while Libby and Gasa moved along in the middle pushing the cattle ahead until they reached the wagon train's camp for the night. The cattle were watered at a small creek then moved behind the circle of wagons.

Libby slid off Gasa behind the freight wagon. Her baby was waiting for her and she nuzzled him then shook her damp coat.

"Give her some water Libby," Jesse called from the family wagon.

Libby led the mare and her colt to the creek. When they had their fill of the cold water Libby took them back to the freight wagon. Jessie was there waiting.

"Libby, you did a real good job finding the strays. I told you Gasa would help you. She is a grand little mare and you are a mighty brave sister to ride her.

Libby smiled and tossed her damp braids back from her face.

At supper Papa sat on the ground next to Libby.

"Libby you did a fine job today and you were brave to ride Gasa. She proved to be a good little cow pony." He reached his arm across Libby's back and gave her a tight hug.

Tears filled Libby's eyes but she squeezed them tight before they could spill down her cheeks.

"I just hung on to Gasa's back and she did all the rest," she said softly.

Libby was very tired. She had helped Little Ben up the mountain and now she helped Mama with the supper as well as help with the cows. When supper was over and dishes washed and Little Ben was tucked into bed in the big tent, Libby at last had some time to herself. She sat outside the wagon listening to the insects singing in the trees. She felt proud of herself. She had been awfully scared but she had ridden Gasa when she was needed. Because Jesse had trained Gasa well, things turned out just fine. This time she didn't disappoint Papa and most of all, she hadn't disappointed Jesse.

THE BARLOW TRAIL

"Ho-oo-ah! The mighty Columbia," Captain Jamison said as the wagon train came within sight of the great river. Libby could smell the damp air. When their wagons rolled up on the bank of the river she could see water that seemed to go on forever before it reached land on the other side. Big waves washed up against the shore. Indians in canoes were paddling across the water, holding up salmon, offering them for sale. There were many families with wagons waiting for a boat or raft to take them down the Columbia. Children scampered around. Cattle and horses milled around the river bank.

"This looks like an ocean and not a river," Jesse said.

"It is a mighty river," Papa said. "We won't be driving the wagons across here."

"All right folks," shouted Captain Jamison. "This is where you have to make a decision. Do you go down the Columbia or do you go ahead to the Barlow Trail and over Mt Hood? Now folks," he continued. "Going down this river is dangerous. You need a guide to get you around rough water. You can hire Indians to take you in a canoe or make a sturdy raft and pray for the best if you choose to take the river route. If not, you have the long, hard journey across Mt. Hood by the way of the Barlow Trail. I end my services here and thank you all for your trust and cooperation. "

"Good luck," voices called.

"Thanks Captain Jamison. Thank you. Thank you."

Papa said, "It's sad to see him go. He is a good man and we will surely miss him. I'm going to look for a boat or canoe to take us down the river. I'm not sure we can make it over the Barlow Trail without a guide."

"I'll stay with you folks if you want a guide. I've been over the territory before. It ain't easy but you can make it if you are careful. I will do it for you for a team o' mules when we get to Oregon City," Redtop said.

"If you think you can find the way it's a deal, Redtop," Papa answered.

"We will go with you," other voices shouted.

"Count on us," Mr. Conners called out.

"May as well get started first thing in the morning," Redtop said. "Get things packed up tonight and find a place to camp where you can get some sleep. May have to leave the river for a distance to get away from this noise and commotion."

Papa drove the wagon back on the trail and found a camping spot. When supper was finished and everything was packed up, Libby crept into the family wagon and into her bed. It had been an exciting day seeing the big Columbia and all the wagons and livestock at the river bank. Mama had traded one of Papa's old shirts for a big salmon fish and it had tasted so good at supper. Nancy came to her bed and the two sisters curled up into their blankets to keep out the cold air and were soon sleeping.

***

Redtop came to their camp very early in the morning.

"Roll out, roll out!" he shouted. "No lagging on this trail. We gotta cover some ground while we have daylight. It's no easy trail we're takin."

There was a cold breakfast of buffalo jerky and bread and water. The families were soon ready to go.

Red Top's shrill call pierced the morning air as he called again, "Roll out!"

The wagons bumped along the rough trail. Libby, Nancy and Mama walked beside them.

"These rocks are surely hard on my feet," Nancy said.

"At least you have some shoe leather left," answered Libby. "Mine is missing half of my shoe soles. When we get to Oregon I am hoping for another pair."

"Chances are Papa will have to make you another pair. I am afraid that new shoes are scarce in Oregon," Mama said.

"But I will still be so glad when we finally get there," Libby answered.

The wagon train traveled over the rough cattle trail that went around the east side of giant Mount Hood with its snow covered peak. The long, hard days of travel had left the gaunt oxen with sore feet and the family with few provisions. The trail over the mountain was steep. It was sometimes necessary to hitch more teams to each wagon to get it over the high, rough places.

"Get that team hitched up with the others Mr. Campbell," Red Top called out.

Will urged Baldy and Clementine forward. Baldy favored one sore foot as he lumbered slowly along. Clementine's ribs stuck out as she strained to pull the heavy load forward.

"That the best team ye got, Campbell ? " Red Top asked.

Papa answered, "That's the best team I've got. They are weary but they have heart."

"Get in there," called out Red Top and he whipped out his long, leather whip making it crack as it skimmed over the oxen's backs. The ox teams inched the wagon forward and it rolled across the rough trail.

"Next wagon up," called Red Top. "Get the teams hitched up. It's slow movin here folks. If we want to get across this mountain before the snow hits us we got to get goin," he shouted.

***

It was dark before all the wagons had been pulled over that part of the rough Barlow Trail. The Campbells set up their cooking fire for supper.

"We have a small piece of bacon and a bit of flour left. Everything else is gone. I'll try to make it last until we get over this mountain. I have been told that there is a farmer who has provisions for sale at the end of this trail," Mama said as she placed the iron spider over the fire.

Sparks flew up from the fire as the bacon started to sizzle. The smell of frying meat filled the air. Libby stood watching. Her mouth watered as she thought about how good the bacon would taste.

“From the looks of those small pieces of bacon we will all have just a taste,” Nancy said.

“I”m as hungry as a big old bear,” said Libby. “Wish I had a big pot of potatoes and some ham to go with it.”

“Wishes are just that Libby. We are not the only family with few provisions. I think everybody on this trail is in the same shape. We’re just hanging on until we reach the end of this journey,” Mama said.

“I know Mama,” Libby said; “ Papa can have my bacon because he is a big man and needs more.”

“We will all take our share and no more; We each need to keep up our strength to cover this rough trail.”

When the family had finished their small bites of bacon and biscuits, Mama and Ben came to the wagon to sleep. Little Ben squeezed in with Libby and Mama and Nancy shared her bed. Papa and Jesse rolled up in blankets and slept outside. There was no room for the tent among so many trees.

***

The next day was a day of struggle. Limbs and logs had to be moved in order for the wagons to move ahead. The weary oxen toiled over rocks and small limbs, finally reaching the very worst part of the trail, Laurel Hill.

Red Top said, "It's a booger of a hill ."

Libby, Nancy and Mama stood at the top of the extremely steep hill. When they looked down they could see loose rocks inside a narrow chute that seemed to go straight down and was just wide enough for a wagon.

"How can we ever get down this terrible hill?" Mama asked. She sat down on the ground and began to cry, her sobs so loud they echoed deep into the thick trees.

Nancy and Libby sat down on each side of her.

"Don't cry Mama. Please don't cry," Libby pleaded."

"Mama, it looks impossible but Red Top will get us there if anybody can," Nancy reassured.

Papa came and put his arms around Mama's shoulders. "You've been a good soldier all along this trip. We need your help to go just a little farther. You can make it. I know you can," Papa said and he took Mama's arm and lifted her up to her feet.

"I will help Mason keep the stock moving," Nancy said. His horses are tired and hungry but they will keep going for awhile."

"The Mules are plain tuckered out. I hope they can last for Red Top to take one team as pay for guiding us," Papa said.

“We have unloaded everything we can but Jesse can’t walk down this hill with his broken leg so he will have to ride in the wagon with Ben,” Mama said.

“All right. Let’s get going,” Papa said. Everybody walks down the hill but Jesse and Ben.”

“Next wagon up.” called Red Top. “Who wants to be first to try this hill?”

“I’ll do it,” Papa answered.

Red Top shouted out orders. “Get busy and cut down a small tree with a trunk six inches or so across. Fasten it to the back axle of your wagon. It will slow the wagon down some. We will have to tie a rope to the wagon then secure it to a tree up here. We can let out the rope slow as the wagon goes down. Get your wheel team hitched up Campbell. Use the ox team and not them excitable mules.”

Papa chopped down a small tree, helped Will drag it to the wagon, and tie it to the back axle of the family wagon with a chain . He then tied a heavy rope around the wagon and fastened it to a strong tree at the top of the hill. He hitched Baldy and Clementine to the wagon.

“All right. Let’s get her movin,” Red Top shouted.

Will urged Baldy and Clementine forward and they moved

over the edge of the steep chute. The tree at the back axle made a swishing sound as the limbs brushed over the loose rocks. Will walked next to the oxen as they strained to keep in front of the wagon.

The oxen slid through loose rock, then suddenly stopped and the wagon slid into their chains. Baldy let out a low bellow when the wagon pushed against him.

"Tighten that rope," yelled Red Top. Too much slack."

The men holding the rope struggled to pull the rope taunt to hold the wagon back.

"The tree is coming loose," Papa shouted.

He hurried down the chute slipping and sliding his way to the wagon. He wrapped the chain around another tree and locked it tight. Will reached for his leather whip and cracked it over Baldy and Clementine.

"Ho!" he called out.

The oxen inched forward and at last reached the bottom of the hill.

Mama and Libby walked down the steep hill sliding down, catching hold of brush and tree trunks to keep from falling. Nancy and Mason rode through the trees with the cattle urging them down the hill.

"Next wagon up," called out Red Top."

Will brought the heavy freight wagon forward. " This one will be a bear," he said.

"We've got a heavy load on here but let's give it a try."

Will and Papa cut another tree and fastened it to the back axle. They tied rope around the wagon then wrapped it around a tree at the top of the hill. Will brought Bright and Roan up and hitched them to the wagon.

"That the best team you got? They look plum tuckered out ," Red Top said.

"The mules are worn out and the other oxen can hardly walk. This is the best we can do," Will said.

"Well, good luck. Ye may not make it in one piece," Red Top said.

Will spoke softly to the oxen. "Get in there Bright . Get going Roan. "

The weary oxen started forward. Their chains squeaked and the limbs from the tree rolled rocks behind the wagon. Will swung his leather whip over the oxen's heads shouting, "Hi! Hi! Get in there Bright. Hey, Roan!"

The oxen inched ahead trying to get away from the big wagon. It suddenly shot forward. The rope around the tree snapped in two. The heavy wagon rushed forward and broke the chains. Bright and Roan scrambled up out of the chute away from the wagon as it swung from side to side, somehow staying upright until the wagon tongue sunk into the ground at the bottom of the hill.

Will sat at the edge of the chute with his head in his hands.

"You all right Will?" Papa shouted.

Will lifted his head."Yep, I made it out of there by a miracle. That wagon would've got me for sure. Them poor old oxen didn't make it I don't expect?." Will asked, and held his head in his hands again.

Papa, Red Top and Mr. Conners came rushing down the hill to the wagon.

"She lost one of the wheels looks like," Papa said.

"Yep," said Red Top but you didn't break an axle. You can get that wheel back in order and that wagon will roll again."

"There's the oxen up there on the bank of the chute," Papa said and climbed back up the hill to reach them. "Bright is all right," he said." "Poor Roan is in trouble, just hobbling on three legs. He reached down and smoothed his hand over the ox's bent leg. "It's broke just below the knee. Poor old fellow," he said and stroked the big ox's back. "We'll have to put you out of your misery."

Mama climbed up to the oxen and looked at Roan's bent leg and asked? "Will you have to put him down?"

Papa looked at her sad face and slowly answered. "The animal can't fend for himself anymore. Bring my gun."

Libby got into the family wagon with Jesse and Little Ben to hide from what they knew would happen.

"I can't stand this Jesse. Roan has worked so hard on this trip. He is a good ox. I don't want anything to happen to him," Libby said and brushed the tears off her cheeks.

"I liked old Roan too Libby, but he is hurting bad and won't be able to find any grass or walk away from here. Put your hands over your ears and you won't hear the gun go off."

Libby bent her head and put her hands tight over her ears. She heard a pop that seemed to come from far away but she kept her ears covered until she felt a tap on her shoulder.

"It's over," Jesse said. "No more Roan anymore.

Libby sat on her bed listening to the voices outside as other wagons came down the hill. She was so sad that the big red ox was now gone. She wouldn't need to wash his dusty face or lead him to water. How could he be here just this morning and now gone forever?

It was dark when Mama came back to the wagon with Papa's gun. "This has been a sad day for us but we are down Laurel Hill. I"ll make supper and maybe that will cheer us up.

For supper Libby, like the rest of the family, poured some bacon grease on a plate and sopped it up with a biscuit. She was so hungry she ate it all in a few bites. She was still hungry and looked around at the empty plates of the rest of the family.

"Is that all, Mama?" she asked.

"It's gone Libby. I wish there could be more."

After supper Libby rolled into her blankets with Little Ben. Her stomach growled and she lay thinking of the good things Grandma made at Sunday dinner. Grandma would make fried chicken, mashed potatoes, green beans, pickles and relish, and for dessert there would be a big apple pie and maybe a chocolate cake. When she went to sleep she dreamed of a wonderful feast with all the good things she liked.

In the morning Papa and Jesse worked on the wagon wheel.

They salvaged some spokes from wagons that had crashed and been abandoned at the bottom of the hill. There was beef stew for nooning. Libby tried not to think about where the beef might have come from. Far back in her memory was the picture of Roan the ox standing by the wagons, quietly chewing his cud. She knew the answer but she really didn't want to think about it.

***

The morning was misty and fog covered the tops of the tall trees. The wagons traveled slowly. Libby walked beside the family wagon. Her feet were cold and the strings that she had tied around her shoes to keep them from falling apart were barely tight and the soles kept flopping as she walked. Nancy was herding the cattle with Mason and Jesse and Little Ben were riding inside the wagon. Mamma led Gasa and walked with Mrs. Connors. Mason's two sisters, Becky and Lydia, rode on Gasa's back. Their shoes were gone and their feet were tender from walking barefoot. The little girls cried from the cold and their empty tummies.

Libby could guess how much their feet hurt when they had to walk. She was glad they could ride Gasa even though she wished she had a ride. She was plenty cold and her feet hurt also. She reached down and gave the strings around her shoes a tug to tighten them again. She brushed rain away from her face and ignored the rumble of her stomach. She was still hungry and wet and cold. She wondered if they would ever reach Oregon City. She could hear the sobs of the girls as they rode on Gasa so she walked closer and asked, "Do you girls know how to sing the song Old Susannah?"

The girls didn't answer but they stopped sobbing, still hanging their heads and sniffling as the rain dripped off their long braids.

"Do you know how this goes?," Libby asked. " I came from Alabama with my banjo on my knee," she sang and clapped her hands in time with her singing.

Lydia raised her head and a tiny smile crept over her lips and she softly sang, "I'm going to Louisiana my true love for to see.

Becky joined in and soon they were all singing, even Mama and Mrs. Connors. They didn't notice the rain and laughed when they could hear their voices echo back to them.

***

They traveled all day in the misty rain, finally stopping for the night when it grew dark. Libby took off her wet coat and shook the water from it. Her clothes were damp underneath too. She hurried to the campfire that Papa had started with some dry kindling from the wagon. She stood with her back close to the fire to dry out the back of her dress.

"Don't get too close to the fire," Mama said. "We don't want an accident."

"Mama, this trip is pure misery. Will we ever get to Oregon City?"

"Of course we will," Mama answered. Mason met a man coming from Oregon City and he said it wasn't far to Foster's Farm. We can get food and rest there.

The Connors family stopped close to the Campbell's camp and shared beef and some biscuits Mrs. Connors baked with her last flour. Libby sat on a fallen log near the fire with Becky and Lydia and told them ghost stories. Little Ben hearing their laughter, came running to join them. They forgot to think about their wet and cold clothes and by the time it was bedtime, they were dry again.

***

The sun shone through the tree tops as the wagons traveled on the next morning. Brown evergreen needles lay in damp clumps on the ground and softened the sound of the wagon wheels as they rolled along. Libby rode Gasa and Lydia and Becky rode in one of the Connors' wagons. The sunshine put everyone in a better mood as they worked their way toward the last part of their journey. As the wagons brushed past the low hanging limbs of the evergreen trees, the smell of pine and fir filled the air. Raindrops on the tips of branches sparkled in the sunlight.

Libby felt warm from the sunlight and she forgot about her sore feet and her worn out dress and shoes. She was glad that she had made friends with Becky and Lydia. They were younger and she wanted to make things easier for them.

"Suddenly she heard something. A sound that she hadn't heard in a long time.

"Mama," she called out. Did you hear that?"

" Yes, Libby that's a rooster from the Foster farm. We should see the farm soon."

The wagons climbed up a steep grade and there below were buildings and fences and pastures. It was the first farm that Libby had seen in a long time. She could hear shouts from the wagons in front and behind. People came running ahead to catch sight of the farm.

At the Foster farm Redtop took the mules, Prince and Toby, as payment for guiding them and said goodby. Papa arranged for a cabin for the night for the family. Mama bought fruit and vegetables from the Fosters. Nancy and Mason drove the cattle into a fenced pasture where there was good grass. Libby put Gasa and her colt there too. Papa paid Mr. Foster for each animal to pasture there.

The cabin Papa rented had no windows or fireplace. Mama built a fire outside and made a supper of fresh vegetables. They tasted so good.

"How long has it been since we had fresh vegetables?" Mama asked."

"It has been too long Mama," Nancy answered.

The family brought blankets and quilts from the wagon and spread them on the floor of the cabin to make a place to sleep for the night. Libby curled up in an old quilt and tried to go to sleep. She kept hearing the mooing of the cows and the rustle of an animal outside their door. It's probably just someone's dog she thought and pulled the quilt tighter. She was warm and for the first time in a long time her tummy was completely full. *Oregon is a good place* she thought. *I am happy we are here at last.*

The next day the Campbell family and the Conners family

started for Oregon City. Papa would look for the right piece of land where they could settle. Libby walked beside the wagon. The Conners sisters walked with her and chatted gaily about what they were going to do in Oregon.

"We are going to have a big garden," Becky said.

" With lots and lots of potatoes and tomatoes and corn and beans," echoed Lydia.

"Yes and lots and lots of pretty flowers," Becky added.

"And maybe some lettuce and radishes," Lydia said.

"Don't you think so Libby?" Becky asked.

Libby took her hands away from her ears when she felt the little girl tug at her skirt.

"Oh, yes, yes, yes," she answered, wishing her ears could take a rest.

The Campbell and Connors wagons pulled up to camp just outside Oregon City. They found a place to put up their tents and Mama, Mrs. Connors and Nancy made supper. Libby sat quietly on the family wagon tongue. She could hear voices coming from a small settlement. There were dogs barking and away in a pasture came the mooing of cattle.

"Oregon at last," she thought. It seemed like a strange place with so many tall fir trees but she was very glad that her family was here at last.

It was two days before Papa came back to the camp. He had looked for land where they could build a house and raise crops.

"I have found land for us," he said. "The Connors will be next to us. They have found two places. One for the Connors family and one for Mason. We will be moving out in the morning to start work on the land.

***

A log cabin was built on the land and the Campbell family no longer had to live in the wagon and the big tent. The log walls were chinked with mud and a big, stone fireplace blazed in one end of one room where the family cooked and ate. Papa and Jesse made a table and chairs and some wooden benches. There was another room where Mama and Papa could sleep and for keeping necessary things. There was a loft upstairs with a wooden ladder reaching from downstairs up to the opening . Here Nancy, Libby, Jesse and Little Ben had pole beds with leather thongs stretched from side to side. Libby folded an old quilt and placed it on top for a mattress . She spread a flannel sheet over it and piled on two quilts to keep her warm.

"It's a good home," she thought and scooted down into her covers.

THE WEDDING

In mid December Mama and Nancy were hurrying about with cooking while Libby was busy putting fresh evergreens and some red berries in the corners of the front room. Nancy and Mason Connors were getting married.

"Do you think this looks pretty?" Libby asked.

Nancy answered, "It is very pretty." .

Nancy is going to have a very pretty wedding," Mama added.

"What smells so good?" Libby asked.

"That's my wedding cake," said Nancy. "It was so good of Mrs. Connors to give us the eggs to make it."

"Yes, and she said I could get two hen from her and then we can have our own fresh eggs," Mama said. "It's time to get the table ready Libby. Get Grandma's big white tablecloth out of the trunk and cover the table. You might put a few pine branches and red berries in a bowl for the table too."

"Mama, do you think I could have a wedding bouquet to carry?" asked Nancy.

"Of course. Libby and I have been gathering wildflowers

since before the frost came. Now we have them dried and in a bouquet for you. "

"Oh, Mama, I should have known you wouldn't forget." said Nancy and she gave Mama a big hug.

"Mama smiled and said, "All right girls, the preacher will be coming soon and he may need breakfast. He has to ride horseback almost twenty miles so he must have left home early. Let's get things finished before he gets here."

Libby lifted Grandma's tablecloth out of Mama's trunk. She spread the white linen over the wooden table and smoothed out the wrinkles. She cut pine branches and red berries and fit them into a small pitcher and placed it in the middle of the table. Then she set out Mama's china plates. These had been packed into the flour barrel to keep them from breaking when they crossed over the trail. Since there wouldn't be enough plates for everyone coming, so she also put out the tin plates they had used on the trail. Mama had made some small dolls with acorn heads and colored leaf bodies so Libby set one in front of every plate.

"That looks very pretty Libby," Nancy called from the fireplace where she was checking the roasting venison. You are handy with so many things now. I am proud of my grownup little sister."

"Let's get things put away now girls," Mama said. "People will be coming in soon."

"I'll sweep up the floor and make sure the chairs and benches are dusted," said Libby.

When the hands on the big clock on the mantel reached ten, the cabin was neat and ready for company. The bouquet on the table was bright and cheery. The little acorn dolls made a spot of color at every plate. The fire in the stone fireplace at the end of the room blazed bright, lighting up the cabin.

"Time to get dressed girls," Mama said. "I will help you Nancy if you need me, and I will get myself ready."

Oh, Mama, I want you to help me look my best on my wedding day," She said, then ran to Mama, threw her arms around her and gave her a tight hug.

"My precious Nancy. My little girl grown up and getting married. I hope you have a wonderful and happy life," Mama said and brushed at the tears that came to her eyes.

"Libby I will need your help too."

"Do you really, Nancy?"

"Of course I do. You are my dependable grown up sister

now."

"I want to be."

"You are going to be my helper when Nancy is gone," Mama said. "You have grown up a lot since we left home to come West. I am awfully glad to have my two girls. They are worth more than I can say."

They walked into the bedroom and Libby smiled when she saw Nancy's beautiful wedding dress spread across Mama's bed. The folds of the blue skirt fell to the floor. The bodice lay across the bed with its lace collar sparkling white around the neck and white edging at the wrist bands. Pearl buttons ran in a row from the neckline to the waist.

"Oh Mama," whispered Nancy, " it is so beautiful. Thank you, thank you for making it and for letting me have the material from your good dress. "

"You're welcome. I want my girl to have a pretty wedding dress and this one you can wear for good after your wedding. I wish you could have had a beautiful wedding gown but now that we are in Oregon, there isn't any place to get one. I think this dress turned out quite nice and it will bring out your dark hair and blue eyes.

Libby reached out and smoothed her hand across the full skirt to feel the soft, wool folds.

"You will look so beautiful Nancy," she whispered.

" Help me get dressed. It will be time for people to come soon. I want to stay in the bedroom until it's time and then I will come out to meet Mason."

Libby brought warm water for Nancy to bathe. When she was dressed in fresh underwear and stockings Nancy lifted the dress up and Libby gathered the folds of the skirt and held them until Nancy could slip the bodice over her head and carefully button the small pearl buttons. She looked in the old mirror that hung from a nail on the wall and adjusted the skirt until it fell in soft folds from her small waist.

"Oh Nancy you look so beautiful," Libby said softly.

"Yes, you are pretty as a picture," Mama said. "Now let me fix your hair."

Mama brushed out Nancy's long, black hair, pulled it back, curled the ends, and pinned them up.

"I think everything is ready, so Libby, let's get Little Ben and ourselves cleaned up," she said.

Libby helped little Ben into trousers Mama had let down

and a shirt made from one of Papa's old ones. She put on a brown wool dress that had once belonged to Nancy.

Papa and Jesse came through the front door dressed in their best trousers and shirts. Mama had cleaned and mended Papa's dark coat and it looked nice even if it was threadbare at the ends of the sleeves.

Jesse walked over to the fireplace, proud and straight. Over his shirt he wore a beautiful deerskin jacket with fringe down each sleeve.

"That jacket suits you fine, Jesse," Papa said.

"I know Papa. I sure thank Mama and my sisters for it. I guess I ought to thank Charlie Martin too since he found it on the trail and gave it back. Wonder if he reached California?"

"I hope so and I hope Liza and her family and the other folks we knew made it through safely."

"Look Papa," Jesse said, glancing out one of the the cabin's front windows. "Isn't that preacher Ross riding up?"

"I believe it is. I'll go out and help him find a place to tie up his horse."

Wagons began to arrive as well as riders on horseback. People crowded into the front room of the cabin to warm themselves by the fire. Libby and Little Ben took their wraps and found a place in the corner of the bedroom where Mama had laid down an old quilt and carefully put them there.

Mama stood at the door in her grey wool dress and greeted the people as they came inside the cabin.

"Welcome, welcome," she said. "Come in and get warm. I know you have had a long trip."

"We did have a long trip and a cold one too," a neighbor lady said.

"We are happy that so many neighbors have been able to come considering how far apart we all are," Mama answered.

Preacher Ross stepped out from the crowded room to stand in front of the fireplace.

Above the hum of voices he said, "All right folks. We have come here today to join two people in holy matrimony. Would the bride and groom step forward?"

Out of the crowd stepped Mason Connors. He was tall and handsome in a dark suit, white shirt, and dark string tie. He walked confidently to stand beside Preacher Ross.

A soft murmur went through the room. "The bride, the bride."

Eyes flew to the bedroom door as Nancy entered the room. She looked beautiful in her dark blue dress. Her cheeks were rosy and her dark hair shone in the light from the fireplace as she walked over to stand by Mason.

The cabin was very quiet as Preacher Ross spoke the wedding vows. With the answer of, "I do," repeated by Mason and then Nancy, the minister said, "I now pronounce you man and wife."

The room filled with the sound of clapping hands and a sharp whistle from Jesse. The minister turned to Mason and said, "Now you may kiss the bride."

There was happy laughter when Mason held Nancy close and kissed her on the lips. Nancy then turned toward the crowd in the room, her cheeks rosy, red and smiled at the good wishes called out to her and Mason.

Mama and Libby brought out the food that was prepared, the potatoes, the jams and jellies, the hot bread, and the roast venison .

Mama invited guests to sit down at the table until it was filled and then asked those left standing to bring their plates, get them filled, and find a seat on the floor.

Libby and Mason's young sisters, Becky and Lydia, put plates on an old quilt Mama had placed on the floor in the bedroom. Libby helped Little Ben find a place to sit down on the quilt with the other youngsters and they ate their wonderful meal.

"Oh, so good," Libby said, as she finished what she had on her plate.

Mason and Nancy cut their wedding cake and it was served to the guests. Nancy then cut a tiny piece, wrapped it in a napkin, and slipped it into Libby's hand. "It's to help you remember me and look forward to your wedding day."

Libby smiled shyly, her cheeks turning rosy. "My wedding?" she questioned. "That must be a long time from now."

"Oh, the time will come sooner than you can imagine."

Libby looked down at her flat chest and pulled at one of her pigtails and whispered softly,
"Married? That must be a million years away."

The food was put away and dishes washed. The big table was lifted up on its side and set against the wall along with the chairs and benches. The middle of the room was now open.

"All right folks," Mr Connors called. We're going to have a little square dancing here. So honor your partners all and let's make the calico crack."

The floor soon filled with couples led by Mason and Nancy. Mr. Connors put his fiddle under his chin and started playing. A neighbor with a banjo joined in and Will started calling the dance.

"All join hands and forward and back. Swing on the corner, swing partners all. Swing corner lady and promenade the hall."

The dancers stepped out then swung around in time to the music, smiling and laughing. The women's full skirts swirled out as their partners twirled them around the room. When the dance was over the men pulled out their handkerchiefs and wiped their damp faces. The women found a place to sit down and moved their hands back and forth in front of their face hoping to stir some air that would cool them down.

"All right now, if you didn't get into that dance, come and join your partner for this next one," Mr. Connors called.

The dancing went on until the ladies brought out coffee and cookies. After a short break it started again.

Libby tried her best to keep her eyes open but she began to close them and nod.

Mama touched her shoulder and said, " Libby, why don't

you go join Little Ben on a pallet in the bedroom, where the other children are asleep?"

"All right Mama," Libby answered and found Little Ben snuggled on a quilt in one corner of the room. She stretched out beside him and reached her arms around him and cuddled up close until she felt warm.

The dancing went on through the night until the sky turned red in the east and light began to creep around the room, waking up Libby. She watched as Mason and Nancy gathered up their gifts and Nancy's trunk and climbed into their wagon. They were going to their small cabin on Mason's land to start their life as Mr. and Mrs. Mason Connors.

As the horses pulling the wagon moved forward, voices shouted, "Good luck! Good luck!"

Libby stood watching and waving. For the first time she felt the loss of her big sister. There would be no more late night story telling, no more sewing sessions, and no one to confide in and ask for advice when she was too embarrassed to ask anyone else. She felt like crying but she knew she should be happy for her sister and Mason. She was supposed to be growing up and responsible. I should not worry so much about myself she thought.

She walked slowly into the cabin, quietly walked to the bedroom and pulled out her quilt bag. She reached inside the bag and took out the piece of wedding cake Nancy had given her. "I'll remember you Nancy and all the good times we had," she whispered. "I will see you sometimes. You won't be that far away. It's just that things will be different."

We're in Oregon now, she thought, and as Papa says, Oregon is a place to build your dreams. She smoothed the napkin that held the wedding cake with her fingers then carefully lifted it up and hid it away at the bottom of her quilt bag. She stood up, placed her hands on her hips, thinking. Oregon is a place for dreaming and I dream that I can learn to shoot a gun and paddle a canoe. I want to have my own horse like Jesse and drive a team like Papa. I want to learn sew and cook and be careful with the things I do like Mama and Nancy. And as Papa says, I want to do my own thinking instead of always following someone else. Most of all, when I am quiet and in a secret place, I want to look deep down inside myself and be proud.

THE END

Little Things

I dreamed big things a long time ago
But I have grown older and now I know
The very best of what life brings
Is our enjoyment of little things
A rose tinted sky from the morning sun
A warm loaf of bread or a cinnamon bun
The jeweled dew in a spider's web
A good night kiss and a nice warm bed
A child's smile and innocent glee
The whispering breeze in a giant old tree
The blue, blue sky and a grassy nook
A crackling fire and a really good book
A patchwork quilt as pretty as you please
And one more day to enjoy all of these

Frances Beryl Vance